The Xpatriot

The Xpatriot

Randall H. Miller

iUniverse, Inc.
New York Lincoln Shanghai

The Xpatriot

All Rights Reserved © 2004 by Randall H. Miller

No part of this book may be reproduced or transmitted in any form or by any means, graphic, electronic, or mechanical, including photocopying, recording, taping, or by any information storage retrieval system, without the written permission of the publisher.

iUniverse, Inc.

For information address:
iUniverse, Inc.
2021 Pine Lake Road, Suite 100
Lincoln, NE 68512
www.iuniverse.com

ISBN: 0-595-33153-X

Printed in the United States of America

This book is dedicated to everyone who encouraged me to write it, especially my mother, Mary Beth Autry, and John Irving (not that one). Thank you for your support, patience, genuine interest and constructive criticism.

The bullet ripped through her head in a split second. The only saving grace of her death was that she died almost instantly. The shooter was either very well trained or very lucky. Either way, she died right in front of him. Within seconds her clothes were crimson. Everything else in his life never seemed to turn out the way it was supposed to. This was no exception. Before he could even think about crying or mourning, before he could go to her to touch her just one more time, he felt his heart harden as his emotional wall rebuilt itself. As the blood started to spill from her lifeless body, he began mentally preparing himself for what he knew she would disapprove of, but what he felt that he must do.

Revenge…

Chapter 1

Camp Freedom Afghanistan

"So I don't get to blow anything up?" asked Blaster, as he juggled three detonators as if he were bored with the mission briefing.

Captain Scott Green ignored him and continued with his mission briefing. "Then, if there are no real questions let's make our final preparations and get ready for insertion. Our mission is simple: we provide security for Alpha Team's raid. If all goes well there should be no shots fired. This should be an in-and-out operation."

"No shots? I'd say that would be a waste of our state-of-the-art training," said Blaster in a low mumble.

"That'll be enough," retorted Scott.

Blaster lowered his head and played with his detonators. He knew better than to push it with Scott during any phase of a mission. It was crunch time and the stakes were high.

Scott walked confidently across the room and sat down near his equipment to check his weapon one last time and run through his mental checklist when Sergeant First Class Frances sat next to him.

"Don't pay any attention to Blaster. He was dropped on his head as a baby."

"I know. It's just immaturity. When they lowered the age and rank requirement we knew we'd get a few."

"You ready?" asked Frances.

"Of course, why wouldn't I be?"

"I'm just asking. It's my job to watch after you officers." Frances smiled, got up and went to check his equipment and quickly pray before mission time.

Frances had been the Team Sergeant for Bravo Team for two years prior to Scott's arrival as the new commander. They immediately took to each other and their mutual respect was obvious to anyone who watched them work together. Scott had needed a strong NCO to help him develop as an officer and Frances had needed a good commander who would let him do his job. It was a perfect fit.

Scott took one last look around the room. The men were making final adjustments to each other's equipment, and checked their rifles for functionality. Scott stood up and snapped his pistol belt closed. Bravo Team stopped talking and looked at their six-foot-one commander with short brown hair and lime green eyes and waited for the word.

"Let's do it."

The airport runway had a blurry haze hovering above it that made it difficult to see clearly. Small aircraft and vehicles quickly turned left and right, weaving in and out of each other's way with well rehearsed precision. Pilots watched their gauges while their crew chiefs watched the soldiers board the helicopters.

Scott led the way as his team slowly walked towards two waiting modified Blackhawk helicopters. Conventional soldiers and their leaders would still be scurrying and making their final preparations. But not these men, they were Special Forces. They had rehearsed their missions, trained through contingencies, checked their equipment for functionality and were waiting for their ride while most troops would have still been reading their operation orders.

Bravo Team had been operating in Afghanistan for almost eighteen months and counting. They were proud of their work, but dreamed of returning to Harley Davidsons, wives and children or, for some, the camaraderie and spiritual support of their churches. Either way, everyone had a reason to get home in one piece. In eighteen months of intense operations there had been some close calls, but no major injuries, just a lot of bumps, bruises and minor fractures. Bravo Team often joked that it had the blessings of Allah to function successfully in a Muslim country.

A crew chief moved ahead of the team so he could direct team members to their respective choppers. One by one they filed off towards the Blackhawks as they had done many times before. Scott would wait and go last, ensuring that everyone on the team got a ride. As he was waiting, he felt a gentle tap on his back and turned around.

"Scott, how are you?" asked Lieutenant Colonel (LTC) McCallister.

"Good sir. What's up?" he replied.

"Change of plans. I have an easy one for you."

"Ok." Scott said as he glanced at his men who continued to take their seats on the skids of the choppers.

"There's a small village just north of your original objective. It doesn't even have a name. Anyway, intelligence reports from above say it might be some kind of a holdout. I'm ninety-nine percent positive that they're wrong. Do me a favor and take a look so I can get them off my back."

"What about the raid mission?"

"I've assigned security to Delta team. Your boys can stand down. You guys deserve a break. Let Delta carry some of the burden that your boys have been carrying since we got here," McCallister said.

Scott glanced back and forth several times between McCallister and Bravo Team. Some of the men stared off into the horizon, mentally rehearsing their missions. Others curiously watched Scott as he spoke with the boss.

"I want you to personally check this place out for me. Take two of your men. Two locals will be waiting to guide and translate. Make sure you bring your demo sergeant. Rusty is giving you a ride," he said as he nodded his head towards the first helicopter, piloted by Chief "Rusty" Callahan. Rusty had more hours in choppers than most people have in the bathroom. He was simply the best and everyone knew it.

"All right sir. I'll take care of it."

"I know you will," McCallister answered with a warm and fatherly smile.

Scott remembered the first time he saw that smile. It was at Camp Mckall, North Carolina. Mckall is a small Special Forces training center located on the outskirts of Fort Bragg. Among other things, it is mostly known as the home of Special Forces Selection and Assessment (SFAS), the mother of all tryouts. Only those who make it through are sent to the Q Course (SF Qualification Course.)

Scott had been a senior First Lieutenant (1LT) in the 82nd Airborne Division when he submitted his application. Most of the other lieutenants encouraged him to his face, but doubted his chances in private. Scott was an outstanding officer in every respect, but the physical requirements for SF were daunting to say the least. Scott was never the strongest or the fastest, but he had one thing that worked to his advantage: he would never quit. Scott could not quit anything. It was impossible for him. He could continue to operate in any environment, under any circumstances and never complain about it.

Candidates had been dropping like flies since day two. The first ones to quit were usually the loudest and cockiest, but not always. Injuries forced others out. Intense stress fractures in the feet, torn knees, broken ankles and pulled muscles were common. The only saving grace of an injury was that you had an open invitation to return and try it again. Quitters could never return. *But who would want to go through this twice?* Scott often thought to himself.

And so it was almost at the end of the third week that Scott came face to face with LTC McCallister for the first time. It was the end of what seemed like a never-ending land navigation course. Candidates navigated from point to point while carrying over one hundred pounds of equipment and weapons. After twelve hours, most thought that they had to be close to the end. The truth is that it never ends, not until the instructors have seen what they need. Scott was lacking in his time between points, but he made up for his deficiency with pinpoint accuracy. Most soldiers would get to where they thought their next checkpoint would be, stop and look around for their marker. Scott would orient himself in the proper direction, estimate the distance and put his head down. Without exception he would walk right to his marker, only occasionally veering off course to negotiate an obstacle.

Point #37 on the course was much different than most. The final 1000 meters was almost completely straight up a steep cliff, the marker planted on top. Scott didn't notice the two figures perched on top of the hill watching him as he approached. It was dark and he was more concerned with his body than with observers.

His feet were swollen to the point where he no longer wanted to take his boots off to treat his feet; he feared he might not be able to get them back on. He was also pretty sure that both ankles were fractured. The rest of his body was badly beaten or broken, but he continued on with admirable perseverance. On his final approach to the marker he fell continuously. Sometimes he landed on his back, sometimes on his side, but his rifle never touched the ground. He occasionally heard a faint chuckle from above but it didn't bother him.

Scott finally reached the top of the hill. The two figures were standing next to the marker about 20 meters in front of him. He straightened himself out and staggered towards them. His canteens had been empty for the past hour and his head was spinning. As the two figures came into focus he tripped and fell face first onto a large stone. Blood splattered and anyone within fifty feet could have heard his nose break.

One of the figures approached. Scott could see a set of boots in front of him as he struggled to return to his feet. LTC McCallister looked him in the eye, but said nothing.

"Excuse me," Scott said softly, as he walked around McCallister to the instructor at the marker. "Alpha two zero."

"Kinda slow two zero. You wanna stop?" the sergeant said, as he held out a small index card with Scott's next direction and distance on it.

Scott resented the question, but managed to shake his head as he took the card. He pulled out his compass, shot his next direction and stuffed a handkerchief into his nostrils as he put his head down and continued the long march.

"Kids got heart, I'll give him that," he said, as Scott's figure quickly blended into the darkness. The faint rustling of leaves and twigs under his feet could be heard for another 30 seconds or so until all evidence of him was gone and the sergeant turned to wait for the next candidates, if they hadn't quit yet.

"Yes he does and that's the most important element," McCallister said.

"Also the toughest to evaluate," the sergeant said without looking up from his clipboard.

"No family you said?"

"Nothing. Parents died when he was a teenager. No brothers or sister, aunts or uncles. Grandparents all either died or disappeared when he was a kid."

"What did the group shrink say about him?"

"Profile is pretty basic. He's mentally strong, probably because of his background. It's tough to shake somebody after they've been through a tragic loss like that. Things can't get much worse. What are you gonna do? Take away their birthday?"

"I like him. He's got something. You can see it in the eyes."

From that day forward, LTC McCallister became Scott's mentor and surrogate father figure. Over the next seven years they became very close. Some of the SF troopers would joke about Scott being adopted by the commander. Scott spent many holidays and special occasions with the McCallister family. They had a bond of trust and mutual respect topped off with a genuine concern for each other. They became like family. It was a given that Scott would be at the McCallister house on Christmas and Easter.

The sound of the Blackhawk brought Scott back to the task at hand. He walked over to the first Blackhawk and explained the mission change. Scott informed Blaster and Frances that they would be going with him and that the others had the night off. The men immediately began unbuckling themselves.

Scott, Frances and Blaster checked each other's equipment and jogged towards the next Blackhawk. They boarded, strapped themselves in and gave the nod to Rusty that they were ready. Rusty winked and smiled, then signaled that it would only be a moment before they would depart.

Blaster was called so for obvious reasons. He was the team demolition sergeant. He could do anything with explosives, but put little effort into the other aspects of soldiering. When he was in the Q Course (Qualification course to become a Green Beret) his only saving grace was his uncanny and natural, almost artistic, ability to employ explosives in any situation. At the end of the course the commanding officer still wanted to fail him for his average marksmanship and attitude, but the sergeants all lobbied to keep him and eventually won. SF soldiers are the elite and their opinions carry a great deal of weight with their superiors. Blaster was gifted in many ways, but sometimes lacked the judgment and maturity that green berets are known for.

Frances was the Team Sergeant, a clean cut father of five children and an unwavering patriot. When he wasn't writing letters home to his family or looking at their pictures, he was reading books about the founding fathers or other influential Americans. Frances was also a very religious man, but never forced his faith on others or spoke of it unless they showed an interest.

Scott did one final check to make sure that his radio communications worked properly. Then he looked up to see LTC McCallister speaking to a man whom he didn't recognize. McCallister had one hand on the man's shoulder and with the other he pointed towards Scott. After another 30 seconds of discussion, the man walked briskly towards the chopper, climbed aboard and strapped himself in next to Blaster. He looked at Green and the rest of the crew and then looked out the doors for the rest of the trip without actually acknowledging anyone.

He was dressed in standard camouflage, but wore no insignia. His dark hair was long, almost civilian, but he was armed and gave the impression that he knew what he was doing. He could have been Delta Force, but it wasn't likely. He would have greeted them. More than likely he was CIA.

The flight took about fifteen minutes before Rusty signaled that they would be at the landing zone in two minutes. Equipment check. Locked and loaded. The Black Hawk landed in unfamiliar terrain with the speed and accuracy that only a Task Force 160th pilot could pull off. The soldiers exchanged looks, but said nothing. One of the trademarks of SF soldiers is that they rarely have to talk while on a mission. They just know.

Scott had always been a good officer, the kind of leader who was approachable and disarming. He was well respected by his peers and superiors, but more importantly, by the soldiers. His team members would follow him anywhere.

Rusty put the Blackhawk down softly and quickly. Scott and the team popped their restraints and exited the craft as they had done hundreds of times before. They shuffled away from the chopper and its forceful rotating blades so Rusty could take off again and disappear until their extraction. Scott could see their Afghani contacts waiting on the edge of the impromptu landing zone.

Scott turned back to make sure Blaster and Frances were still with him when he noticed an extra person following closely behind them. It was the man from the chopper.

"Can I help you with something?" Scott asked firmly.

"Nope. I'm just along for the ride."

"If you're looking for public transportation, we aren't it."

"Maybe not but you'll do for now," He said, as he removed his sunglasses to clean them with a small white handkerchief.

Scott grabbed him by the arm firmly and looked into his eyes. They were about the same height but Diablo had a much slimmer build and Scott guessed that he was in his late thirties. Both of them stared at each other for several seconds. Scott held his gaze and studied his eyes. The eyes never lie. People can change their facial expressions. They can move their brows, cheeks, lips and noses but nobody can change their eyes. And that is where the truth always lies.

"Relax Captain Green. I'm one of the good guys," the man said, as he extended his hand.

"I'll be the judge of that. Who are you?"

"Sorry I didn't have time to introduce myself before. I'm Diablo."

"And?"

"And I'm just here to observe. That's what we do."

"Who's we? CIA?"

"Something like that. I work for a classified division of Homeland Security and that's all you need to know," he said with a straight face and enough force to discourage any more questions.

"Fine. Just remember that this is my mission and I don't need a babysitter."

Diablo chuckled and shook his head. "Unfortunately that decision isn't up to you, but whatever helps you sleep at night, Scotty." Nobody had called him Scotty since high school. *Who the hell does this guy think he is?*

The two Afghani contacts smiled, nodded and extended their hands as Scott and the others approached. Their English was broken, but sufficient. Their mere presence with the patrol would usually help to calm the villagers during routine sweeps like this. The misinformation spread by radical Islamists throughout the Muslim world was often hard to overcome. Soldiers of the Great Satan were never to be trusted. Killing them is the ultimate praise that a Muslim man can give to Allah. Scott always wondered how the U.S. was able to recruit such guides and liaisons. It's probably a combination of things, including the almighty dollar, which finally swayed these men to help the infidels.

The contacts lead them to a small scale model of the village and with a large stick they pointed to their current location. The village was small. It consisted of approximately twenty to thirty small structures in the shape of an oval about the size of two football fields.

"Had any problems here?" Scott asked one of the guides.

"No Sa. Farmers here," he replied, as he pointed to the field full of sheep and a few goats.

"No guns?"

"No Sa. No, no. No guns."

Scott looked into his eyes and asked again. "No guns?"

"No, no, no. Peaceful farmers all."

"Ok," Scott said. His warm smile comforted the guide who was obviously nervous around soldiers, but probably needed the money.

"Ok. We'll start from here. Frances, you take our friend Diablo here and head around the village counterclockwise. I'll take Blaster and go clockwise. When we meet on the other side we'll walk through the center together and call it a day," Scott instructed.

There were nods of approval from everyone in the group and soon the two parties started slowly patrolling and looking, each taking an Afghani guide with them. Scott led the way, but made sure to walk side by side with his guide, attempting to display solidarity. The locals, alarmed by the loud sound of the chopper, were slowly trickling into the street. Others peered cautiously out their windows and doors, but all were curious.

Blaster trailed behind Scott and the guide, dragging his feet and occasionally kicking rocks as if to announce his boredom. He looked at some of the villagers as they patrolled by the front of their houses, but never changed his expression. They returned his empty stares, another diplomatic opportunity lost.

"Blaster, why do you go out of your way to broadcast your feelings?" Scott asked.

"No reason. Just a gift I guess."

"Well do us all a favor. Try to remember that we're in somebody else's house, watch your manners and get your feet off the table."

"Roger," Blaster said, accepting the fact that he had annoyed Scott, as he had done many times before. His opinion of his commander overall was favorable. He just wished Scott would show a bit more of his warrior side and not always be so accommodating to the Afghanis.

Scott and the guide scanned the scene. Nothing was out of the ordinary. This appeared to be just another poor village in a poor country riddled with corruption, hatred and despair. Some of the villagers smiled and Scott returned the courtesy. Others looked at the trio as invaders of privacy and infidels with no business in a Holy Land. Those were the hearts that could never be won over by U.S. forces no matter how great the deed. Anything that comes from the occupiers is tainted.

They had begun their patrol on the southeast side of the village and were now at the Northwest corner. Small buildings of various heights spotted the perimeter. The guide stopped and asked if he could stop for a moment to empty his boot. Scott laughed to himself and nodded his approval. Somewhere along the line a set of GI standard issue desert combat boots had ended up on the young man's feet. The boots had no laces. He had removed them and tied them together to use as a belt, explaining why he had a boot full of sand. Scott sat down on a large rock and pressed the handset of his compact, secure radio. The line was internal and secure so there was no need for formality.

"Frances, you there?" he said clearly into the handset.

"Roger. What's up?"

"Nothing. Anything interesting there on your end?"

"Nope. Just the usual blank stares."

"I'll take blank over resentment any day."

"I hear ya. Me too."

"Ok. I'll see you on the other side."

Scott then reached down to his radio and changed the frequency so he could check in with LTC McCallister.

"Freedom six this is Bulldog six, over."

"This is six. Talk to me Scott," McCallister answered.

"Not much to report....small, poor village of farmers...nothing special...should be done within an hour or so....report to follow, over."

"Ok. You can submit your report when you get back. Finish your patrol and return ASAP...no need to wear out our welcome. Rusty needs fuel and some serious maintenance on his bird, so I'm sending him back for you now."

"Roger, anything further? Over."

"Negative, out," McCallister said, as he terminated the transmission.

Blaster whistled to himself and paced as he pretended not to listen to Green. He was always up for excitement, but dreaded the tedium of intelligence gathering and security sweeps. Scott was opening his mouth to speak when something caught his eye.

Next to one of the smaller buildings was a corral with five or six sheep in it. The entire area was fenced off to keep them in, but the building was otherwise unremarkable. There were no people visible. The guide, who was watching Scott examine the building, quickly finished emptying the sand from his boots and jumped to his feet.

"Ok, Sa. Ok now. We go." he said with a forced smile.

"In a minute," Scott said, as he rose to his feet and slowly walked towards the corral. He walked from right to left, looking up and down as he moved. *Why does this seem so strange?* He turned to look at the large flock of sheep grazing freely in the desert adjacent to the village and then back at the coral.

"What's so special about these six sheep?" Scott asked his guide.

"No understand. Special?"

"Why are these six in a special area with a fence while the other eighty or so roam free?"

The guide appeared to be searching for an acceptable answer when he finally replied, "To keep them in." It was a statement, but his lack of confidence was obvious and gave his words the impact of a question.

"To keep them in? Why?" Scott pressed on.

"I am sure they are pets for the children. They keep them here to keep them from getting out," he said, as his English miraculously improved.

"Maybe they're here to keep others from getting in."

Scott reached for his radio and called for Frances. Before going any further it would be wise to consolidate the team.

"Frances, you there?"

"Yes. And I'm alone."

"What do you mean?"

"Diablo stayed with me for the first five minutes then decided to venture out on his own. I'm almost at our meeting point so I sent the guide to go find him and keep him out of trouble. No idea where he is but I should be at your location in a minute or two."

"Ok. He's a big boy. Maybe it's a blessing. Do me a favor and pick up the pace a little bit. I'll wait for you on the Northwest corner."

"Roger. On the way."

Scott replaced the handset on his belt and walked to the edge of the corral. *Hundreds of sheep roaming freely…Except these one…Why keep them in?…Or is it to keep others out?…Or us out?…Think…Think.* And then he saw something even stranger, the remnants of two tire tracks inside the corral. An attempt had been made to cover them up hastily. It looked as if someone had merely kicked sand on the tracks, but the shape and outline was undeniable. These marks came from a car or truck.

Scott examined the lines and noticed how they stretched from the chest high fence that he was standing against all the way to the small shack. The tracks disappeared at the base of the barn as if the vehicle had driven right through the wall. *Interesting.*

"Everything ok, Captain Green?" asked the guide.

"Just fine. We're gonna wait for the others to meet us here before we continue."

"Why don't we keep walking and meet them?"

"Because I'm going to take a closer look at this house."

"But…"

Scott put up his hand and motioned for him not to speak. "Just sit tight buddy. Let me do my job and I'll be on my way. Nothing to worry about."

"Ok, ok. No problem. Trying to help," he said with a forced smile.

Scott looked into his eyes. *This guy is hiding something. The eyes never lie.*

Frances arrived within five minutes. He was walking quickly and apologized as he arrived.

"Sorry. My guide isn't back yet. He's still looking for Diablo."

"It doesn't matter. Anyway, here's the situation." Scott explained and Frances immediately shared his suspicion.

Scott grabbed the top of the fence and pulled firmly. The entire fifteen foot wide end of the fence popped forward. He looked at Blaster and Frances.

"That was easy," Scott said.

"Look. It's hinged on the side. The whole gate must open up. Why would you need that? These nasty critters ain't that big," said Frances.

"No, but it has to be this big if you want to get a vehicle through," Scott offered.

Scott and Frances entered the corral while Blaster remained on the outside to cover them. They weaved through the sheep and approached the outer wall of the barn. It was made with flimsy wooden planks slapped together both vertically and horizontally. The person who made this barn was either sloppy or intentionally wanted it to look undesirable.

The side of the building opened as easily as the gate to the corral when Frances pulled at the far right side.

"Bingo," he said.

"Be careful. We don't know if anyone is in there. I'm thinking we should call for backup," Scott said.

"I can see inside. It's completely empty."

"Ok. Open it up but be careful."

Frances swung the side of the barn open and he walked inside. "See? I told you. It's empty." Just as the last words left his mouth a young boy of seventeen or eighteen years old who had been cowering in the corner rushed past Frances and made a break for the door. Scott grabbed the boy by the shirt. The frail garment immediately ripped and Scott stood holding a piece of the shirt in his hand. The boy jumped the fence and ran into the center of the village with the agility of a gymnast. When Scott turned around he noticed his Afghani guide had been talking to Diablo when the boy appeared and disappeared. The guide seemed unsurprised when the boy made his escape.

"Go after him!" Scott commanded, as he pointed in the general direction of the village.

The guide looked at Diablo first then broke into a half jog in pursuit of the boy. Diablo's facial expression did not change as he continued to watch Scott and Frances. Blaster stood motionless between Diablo and the barn, quickly rotating his head back and forth between the two so he wouldn't miss anything.

Scott and Frances entered the apparently empty barn and looked around.

"Empty," said Frances.

"Now yes. But, before there was a vehicle in here," Scott said, as he pointed two tire tracks, fully intact on the floor of the barn. As he pointed, he tapped the butt of his rifle on the floor. It made a peculiar hollow sound. He stopped, looked to make eye contact with Frances and then tapped again, but harder.

"Does that sound like desert sand to you?" he asked.

"No. Probably some kind of hidden storage," Frances replied.

Scott peered out of the barn and saw Diablo standing next to Blaster, neither of them speaking. The guides had yet to return with the boy and maybe never would. Frances was scanning the ceiling of the barn for more irregularities and noticed a primitive looking pulley system. He pointed to it.

"Some kind of system for raising sheep you think?" he asked.

"Why would you want to raise a sheep?" Scott countered.

"I don't know. I'm just thinking out loud. What else would you use it for?"

"Cargo," Scott answered. "Raising cargo to load onto the back of a truck."

"What kind of cargo?"

"Who knows? Maybe farming stuff, maybe not."

"Weapons, you think?" Frances asked.

"Possibly, but let's look around before we assume anything."

Scott began to walk in small circles on the inside of the barn. It was just wide enough to fit one oversized pickup truck with an extra five to seven feet on either side. He kicked at the sand covered floor as he walked and searched. He was almost done searching on the east side of the barn and made one last kick at the sand when the tip of his right boot caught something.

Frances came over to join him and they both began to kick the sand to the side using both feet. When finished they had uncovered a trap door approximately ten feet by ten feet. One side had hinges and the other a large handle, which Scott had accidentally kicked when he was searching.

"The Presidential suite?" asked Frances.

"I doubt it," Scott answered.

"Probably farm storage," said Diablo, standing directly behind Scott.

Scott turned to face him. Their eyes met again. Scott liked him less and less as the day grew older.

"Yeah, maybe this is where they store the sheep's winter clothes," Scott said, as he turned away from Diablo and waved Blaster in.

"Frances and I will pull security from the side. Blaster, take the rope from the pulley system, stand off to the side and open the doors when I tell you to. Make sure everybody is out of the way before we do it," Scott instructed.

"Maybe it's booby trapped," Blaster immediately retorted.

"I doubt it. This place wasn't meant to be found. They're hiding something that they want to protect. Rigging it with explosives could damage the cargo in addition to any intruders," Scott said.

"How can you be so sure Scott?" Diablo asked

Scott had been kneeling, but stood up straight before answering Diablo.

"Stick around and I'll prove it to you," he said, as he waved his arm for Blaster to work faster. Blaster had been working slowly, looping the pulley system through the door handle with one hand as he watched the interaction between Diablo and Scott.

Frances and Scott both stood off to the side of the door and held their mini M16's with laser sights at the ready position. They were locked and loaded and ready for any surprises. Diablo stood close to them but did not pull his Heckler and Koch USP 9MM from his Velcro holster.

"Ready?" Scott asked, as he looked at Frances.

"Ready."

Scott nodded at Blaster to lift the door. Blaster didn't know how heavy the door would be. Pulling too little could open it only halfway. He decided that too much would be better. He grasped the rope high above his head with both hands and pulled with all of his strength.

The door opened with such force that it flew off of its hinges, slammed against the wall and finally fell flat on the floor of the barn. Nobody moved. Besides the sound of the door crashing into the wall, the barn was silent. The villagers who had been watching from outside had disappeared. Scott and Frances stood still with their weapons aimed at the opening in the floor. Nothing happened. They waited for several moments until Scott broke the silence.

"Cover me."

Frances nodded. Scott glanced over at Blaster who was now standing next to Diablo.

"You too," he instructed Blaster.

Blaster removed his rifle which was slung across his back and aimed the barrel at the opening in the floor. Scott did the opposite and slung his rifle across his back. Then he reached down to his belt and removed his flashlight.

He crouched down as low as he could and approached the opening with extreme caution. Before he was close enough to see inside, he grabbed a rock from the sandy floor and tossed it lightly. The rock landed with a thud. There were no other noises from the hole. *Ok. No noises. No hissing. No snakes. I think. Unless they're highly disciplined snakes. Not likely.* Scott waited a few more seconds before advancing close enough so that when he turned on his flashlight it was able to illuminate the majority of the opening.

He crouched on the floor of the barn and stuck his head into the opening to get a clear look. The flashlight revealed a pit approximately ten feet deep with the same horizontal dimensions as the trap door. There also seemed to be solid flooring. There were what appeared to be shelves against the walls on all four sides, but Scott couldn't see what was on them.

Blaster continued to cover from the other side of the barn when Frances slowly inched forward and kneeled next to Scott.

"What do you think?" Frances asked.

"Storage facility for something that they don't want advertised."

"Want me to take a closer look?"

"Yeah, go ahead."

Frances slung his weapon across his back, located a small ladder that was attached to the side of the hole and slowly climbed down as Scott provided light for his descent. When he reached the bottom he stomped both of his feet.

"Solid flooring. They put some time into constructing this," Frances said.

He removed his flashlight from his belt and shined it on the shelves. He rotated around 360 degrees before stepping forward to look closer. Scott could see him pick something up for a closer look.

"Well, well, well. What have we got here?"

"Let me guess, sheep food?" Scott said.

"Not exactly, here catch," Frances said, as he tossed a small package up to Scott for his examination.

Scott caught the small parcel with his left hand and then rose to his feet. The package was tightly secured with several layers of duct tape. He reached into his pocket and removed a small knife that he generally used for slicing his food. He made a small incision about three inches long and squeezed the bag so he could see the contents.

The small opening released a smell that Scott had not experienced since high school, freshly processed hashish. He had discovered a hiding place of the very lucrative underground drug trade.

"How many of these are there Frances?"

"There are about five hundred of those but this other side has a different flavor."

Frances picked up a hefty-sized trash bag and emptied it on the floor. It was full of poppy plants used to make opium, heroin and other narcotics.

"I thought the Taliban outlawed this stuff when they took power?" he asked.

"They did. The majority of the country's crop was eliminated. They must have felt the financial crunch. This country used to supply seventy or eighty percent of the world's opium supply," Scott answered.

"Well it doesn't qualify as weapons or terrorists. What do we do with it?"

"I don't know. Do me a favor and get a quick count of it all and then hop out. I'm going to call the Colonel to report it and get some more guidance."

Scott retrieved the radio handset from his belt and walked out of the barn. Diablo was outside now and was finishing his own conversation on his handheld SATCOM radio. Scott deliberately ignored him and walked towards the rock from where he first noticed the peculiarity of the barn. He pressed the handset and spoke clearly.

"Freedom six this is Bulldog six, over," he said. Then he released the button and waited for several seconds. There was no reply.

"Freedom six this is Bulldog six, over," he repeated.

Scott was perplexed. *What's the deal here? Everything was working fine before. If something can go wrong it will. Murphy's Law.*

As he continued to try contacting LTC McCallister on the radio, he heard the unmistakable sound of Rusty's Blackhawk approaching the landing zone on the other side of the village. Frances was dusting himself off as he exited the barn.

"Frances, do me a favor and try to get the Colonel on Rusty's radio. This one isn't working, maybe it's not charged. Give him a spot report and request guidance."

"Roger."

"Let's do this quickly, we don't know if we're going to get any visitors."

"Right."

Frances started jogging through the sandy outskirts of the village on his way to the chopper. Scott put his radio back on his hip and crossed his arms in front of his chest as he looked at Diablo and Blaster.

"What do you think?" Blaster asked.

"I think this is a temporary storage facility between the lab where they make this stuff and their point of distribution. We've been in this area of operations for eighteen months and this village has never popped up on the radar screen. That means that they have kept it pretty darn quiet. Unfortunately, it also means that everyone in this village knows about it," Scott said.

"And?" added Diablo.

"And I'll wait for guidance from above, but if I am unable to get it, I'll just blow it all. I don't think we'd be doing anybody any favors by dragging the entire village through interrogations and trying to find the source or destination. That's not our primary mission. We're here to find terrorists, but I can't just leave it alone."

"Why not?" asked Diablo.

"Why not? Because this stuff will undoubtedly end up on the street in the U.S. or in Europe. Personally I could care less if people want to do drugs, but that doesn't mean I have to enable them," Scott said firmly.

Diablo removed his sunglasses and looked at Scott as he had done before. His eyes were dark, almost black. "I agree about the interrogations, but do you think we'll make any friends by destroying it?" he asked.

"Well Diablo, WE won't be doing anything," Scott said, stressing the WE part. "You're just here to observe. Besides, wouldn't WE be doing Homeland Security a favor?" he asked, again putting emphasis on the word we.

"Indirectly, yes, but when you look at the big picture, we may do more harm than good."

"WE will be doing neither. This mission is mine and furthermore..."

Diablo cut him off. "Yeah, yeah, yeah I get your point Scott. Listen, we're walking on egg shells in this country as it is. They're tolerating us because the Taliban made their lives worse, however, we should consider certain tribal traditions before we go blasting away."

Scott rolled his eyes and then refocused them on Diablo. "Don't start. You're here to observe, not advise or recommend or contribute or anything else. I don't report to you. In short, you didn't hire me, you can't fire me."

"Maybe he's right," interjected Blaster. "What would it hurt if we just left quietly? You've seen the look on some of these addicted farmers. Half this stuff will be smoked before it can be exported."

Scott turned and faced Blaster. His blood started to boil. Scott had spent a long time counseling Blaster on keeping his mouth shut when he should be listening, now he was taking sides with someone outside of the team. There are many forgivable sins, but disloyalty is not one of them.

"Blaster, go to the chopper and tell Frances I said to call for backup. These villagers are too quiet. God knows how they're planning to react."

"You really think we need it? If you think it might be dangerous why don't we just leave and come back when we have enough security?"

"Just do it. Besides, do you think this stuff would be here when we return?"

"Whatever," Blaster said immaturely, as he turned and headed for the chopper. Scott made a mental note of his insubordinate attitude and would address it after the mission as he had done too many times before.

Scott and Diablo stood toe to toe in front of the barn. They stared into one another's eyes until Scott broke the gaze and reentered the barn. He stood over the drug cache and thought to himself. *What's the dollar value of all this stuff? How long will it be until the owners come to claim their product?*

"Scott, why don't you just walk away? Let it go and save yourself the trouble," Diablo said, trying deliberately to speak in a soothing and convincing tone.

"Buddy, stop blowing in my ear."

"Seriously though, screw this place. You've done your time. A successful command over here like yours is sure to put you on that Major's list. Hey, I may even be able to put in a good word for you."

Scott turned to face him again. "Look buddy, I don't know who you are and in case you haven't noticed I really don't care. As for pinning on Major, I'm not even sure if I want it. Desk jobs have never appealed to me. But one thing I am sure of is this…I don't like you."

Diablo took a step forward, placing his face only inches from Scott's. "Listen to me Captain. I can handle the heat. I can even handle the scumbags who inhabit this God forsaken land, but I won't take this kind of crap from a small time wannabe like you."

"Wannabe? The last time I checked I was in command of this operation. You're the one who wants to be."

"I'm telling you now, you aren't gonna blow this product," Diablo said defiantly.

"Product? Is that what you guys call it now? What ever happened to contraband or better yet poison?"

"Just accept it now. I can go so far over your head it'll spin."

Scott turned his head from side to side surveying the inside of the barn. "Maybe, but right now we're the only ones here."

"I'll stop you if you try to blow it."

"You mean like this?" Scott said, as he pulled an incendiary grenade from the back of his belt and held it over the hole in the earth. "Why wait for Blaster when I can just blow it right now? You gonna stop me? Do you really care about this stuff that much? And if so, why?"

"Who are you to question me? Nobody, that's who."

Nobody? I'm nobody? Who the hell is this guy? And why should I care?

It takes a lot to make Scott angry enough to fight, but for some reason Diablo was an overachiever in this area. Scott dropped the grenade onto the sand floor, stepped forward and with both hands pushed Diablo in the center of his chest sending him stumbling back several feet.

Amazingly, he didn't go down. Even more amazingly, he was able to pull his pistol and draw a bead on Scott faster than he had ever seen. They both stood motionless for several seconds until Diablo spoke. He seemed to be searching for the right words.

"You just crossed the line Scott. Trust me. You're in over your head on this one. I will kill you. You are obstructing official business of the U.S. Government. As a military officer this could easily qualify as treason, a capital offense. And you're looking at the judge, jury and executioner. I'm telling you right now, for the last time, walk away. Walk away, this never happened."

"I have a better idea. Why don't you put the gun away, come over here, get down on your knees and kiss my ass?" Scott said, in a sarcastic but determined tone.

"Have it your way kid. I tried to help you."

Diablo raised his pistol and pointed it at Scott's head. Scott could see the red glow of the laser sights just above the barrel. He could see Diablo's chest inflate as he took his final breath before slowly exhaling and gently squeezing the trigger, the mark of a professional shooter.

Before Diablo could exhale completely, the impact of Frances' boot to the side of his chest knocked the wind completely out of him and sent him flying against the far wall of the barn. The gun discharged loudly. Scott felt a sharp pain in his shoulder and dropped to the ground.

Frances immediately followed up by pouncing on Diablo and trying to subdue him. Diablo had the advantage as he was not wearing any bulky equipment to slow him down. Scott heard the gun discharge again and was able to lift his head to see the exit hole in Frances' back as it quickly turned red from the flow of blood. Diablo had shot him through the chest at close range.

Scott used all of his strength to sit up. The pain in his left shoulder was unbearable. He looked down and grabbed his left hand and forearm to make sure they were still there. It felt as if his entire left arm had been blown off. He looked down and saw that he was sitting in a pool of his own blood. If was flowing like a faucet. The Mini M16 strapped to his back was unreachable. He tried to apply pressure to his left shoulder with his right hand as he looked over at Frances.

Diablo was standing now and Frances had managed to roll onto his back. He was still alive. His heavy breathing was getting quicker and quicker. Diablo dusted himself off, took a step forward and raised his pistol again. Scott could see the red dot as it hovered on Frances' forehead.

"Adios," Diablo said, without any emotion whatsoever.

"God forgive you," Frances said, in a barely audible whisper as he looked up from the sandy floor of the barn and into Diablo's eyes.

"No!" screamed Scott. But it was too late.

The thunder of the final round echoed in Scott's head. He closed his eyes and he fell back onto the ground. The combination of massive blood loss and the emotional shock of seeing Frances executed was too much. As Scott slowly drifted into unconsciousness, the last thing he saw was Diablo standing over him, followed by a bright red light in his eyes.

Chapter 2

U.S. Army Medical Center Classified Location

Scott woke up in a military hospital. Not the typical kind that most think of. The days of the MASH 4077th are over. Army hospitals have it all now. They have air-conditioning, dining areas and can deliver babies. The young orderly in the room looked a bit too young to be a doctor.

"How am I?" Green asked.

"You alive ain't you?"

Scott looked down at the oversized bandage that extended from the top of his left shoulder all the way down past his elbow. He had several IVs attached to his right arm and the bed was surrounded by medical monitoring equipment that he had never seen before. The room was large but bare. There were no wall hangings or decorations, only white walls and a white tiled floor.

"Mild, medium or barbeque?" Scott asked, referring to the severity of the wound.

"That depends on your 'spective. I seen a lot worse come through here, but I seen a lot better too," the orderly said with a smile, exposing his gold front teeth.

"Please tell me you're not my doctor?"

"Nope, I'm just the brutha who washed your nasty ass."

"Ok. Just checking."

"Yeah. You had some kinda accident on the range. Leave it to an officer to wander onto a live range. No offense."

"What range?" Scott couldn't recall any ranges close to the village in Afghanistan.

"Longstreet," the orderly replied.

Longstreet? The only Longstreet area that I know is on Fort Bragg. That's quite a trip from the Middle East. No way. Not possible.

"Bragg?" he asked.

"Uh…yeah. Do you know any other Longstreet areas? No wonder you got lost. No offense."

"What happened?"

"Don't know bro. But you must have a daddy in the Senate cuz' you got the best care and your own security."

Security? Why would I need security in the U.S.? On Fort Bragg? It's the home of the Special Forces, the Eighteenth Airborne Corps, and Delta Force. Fort Bragg soldiers are the world's largest street gang. Why would I possibly need security?

"Good morning. Billy, let me talk to Captain Green in private for a minute please," said a well dressed man in an expensive suit and shiny wingtips as he entered the room and stood holding the door open for the orderly to exit. Billy nodded his disinterest and left to smoke a cigarette on the roof of the building.

The man closed the door and walked over to the side of Scott's hospital bed. He was tall and lean with short and thinning gray hair. Scott recognized him from somewhere, but could not remember exactly. He unbuttoned his suit jacket and pulled up a chair.

"How do you feel, Scott?"

"Groggy and confused. Care to fill me in or do I have to wait for the book?"

"They told me you were quick witted, but let me start by saying there won't be any books about this one."

"Why's that?"

"Scott, I'm Senator Roland Burke from Vermont, Chairman of the Intelligence Committee in Congress and we need to talk."

Scott now recognized the Senator from his days at Norwich University, a small military college in central Vermont. Burke had been a frequent visitor and leadership speaker for the Corps of Cadets. They had spoken on several occasions when Scott was an aspiring officer. And now they were face to face again, but in a much different scenario. *This is weird.*

"I'm not quite sure…"

"Just listen first and then you can talk. Your mission in Afghanistan is classified and will remain so indefinitely. Once you got back to the base camp, we stabilized you and immediately flew you here to Fort Bragg for the best medical attention available. Your wound was pretty bad. You lost a significant amount of blood and have been drifting in and out of consciousness for the past few days. You'll probably be tired for a few more weeks. Listen closely. Black Ops doctors are not privy to mission information. They just treat wounds. Not a lot of patient interaction for them but they're also the only docs in the military who get bonuses."

Scott wanted to groan out loud as Burke continued. *Where is he going with all of this?*

"Either way, your doc will be in here in a minute to check you out. Answer his questions, but remember your mission is classified. Then we'll go through some debriefing and relax."

"Doesn't sound too relaxing to me."

"I'll see you next door."

As Senator Burke left the room, Dr. Rosen entered. He was a short man in his late 40's. He asked no questions. Without any eye contact whatsoever he explained the antibiotic and pain reliever dosages for the next few weeks. He spoke to Scott without ever looking him in the eyes. *This is the worst bedside manner I've ever seen.* Dr. Rosen signed off on Scott's chart and walked quickly towards the door. Scott raised his good hand and spoke.

"Doc? Doc? Can I ask a question?"

Dr. Rosen turned around and looked at Scott. He nodded his approval, but said nothing.

"Will I regain one hundred percent use of my shoulder?"

"No," Dr. Rosen replied, without any emotion whatsoever. Then he turned back towards the door and quickly exited. Two civilians had been waiting in the hallway and immediately came in with a wheel chair.

"Ready to go Captain Green?" asked the larger of the two.

"Depends on where we're going, but I suppose that any place is better than Afghanistan."

"Captain Green, we're just couriers. We aren't privy to any mission information. Our job is to take you to the tank next door."

"The Tank? Sounds like a charming place. Do I have a choice?"

"No, but the food is good and I promise nobody will shoot at you," he said with a warm grin.

Ok. Don't shoot the messengers.

They loaded Scott into the wheelchair with ease and immediately they were on their way. What Scott had originally thought was the inside of a swanky mobile hospital was actually the Delta Force all purpose clinic. Their facilities and capabilities are among the best in the world, even able to perform organ transplants. Scott knew where he was almost immediately because he could see the fences and raised terrain all around the perimeter. But the biggest hint of all was what the military calls relaxed grooming standards. There weren't any of the usual high-and-tights haircuts that cover most military posts. This looked like a small town of civilians.

Burke was waiting when Scott arrived. The Tank is the most secure part of the Delta compound. Nothing could come up the toilet in this building without sounding the bugle. There were only a few other people in the room. One or two of them managed to at least look up and say hello as Scott was wheeled in.

"Well Scott. You were able to uncover the hub of one of Afghanistan's largest drug rings. That's quite an accomplishment, even if it was by accident, as you say."

"As I say? You mean that's under speculation?"

"It's just part of the whole process Scott. That's why we're here, for the truth."

"The truth is that I was ordered to patrol a village I had never heard of or been to. It wasn't my idea. I just do what I'm told. I also watched Diablo kill one of my best men in cold blood. If I ever see him again, I will not hesitate to…"

"Stop right there Scott. You don't want to say anything foolish about a highly decorated intelligence operative who probably saved your life."

"Saved my life? The bastard shot me. What the hell are you talking about? I didn't want to go to that village. I went where I was told."

"So you're suggesting that perhaps there is an issue with your chain of command? LTC McCallister is your CO, right? Did he send you to the objective?"

"Yes but no. I'm not implying anything. I think we stumbled upon something that nobody ever thought we'd find. It was purely accidental. The Colonel sent me there, but mentioned that he was tasked to do so by Intel?"

"Maybe Scott, but I'll agree with you about LTC McCallister, he has been a model soldier and commander for the past 20 years," Senator Starling said, as he raised his voice, lifted his head high and looked at the others in the room, emphasizing his point.

"The other Team members I'm not so sure about," he continued.

"What are you talking about?" Scott said defensively.

"Your demolition sergeant checked out ok, but your weapons sergeant has some interesting financial issues to explain. Unfortunately, he is dead and we'll never know the whole truth. With these types of things all we can do is try our best to investigate. Inevitably, the family claims ignorance and we chase our tails. This case probably died with SSG Frances. More than likely nothing will be proved and the family will make out with one hundred percent of his SGLI (serviceman's group life insurance) and his pension."

"Make out with it? I know Frances' family and nothing will be able to replace their father. He was a good man. A very religious man and he walked his talk."

"Well Green, I'm not her to piss on a man's grave. But I'm not here to plant flowers on it either. I can also tell you that the religious gimmick is one of the most widely used fronts I've ever seen. There's something about a religious person that other people fear, it makes them reluctant to ask questions. It makes them very careful about what they say and do in their presence. They drop their guard and common sense in order not to offend. Fortunately, there are people like me in positions to sniff them out."

"But Sergeant Frances was killed by Diablo, I saw him…" Scott tried to interject.

"Just listen, Scott. There's been over a quarter million dollars in cash deposited to his accounts in the past year. Explain that to me. How does a man who makes barely forty grand a year, is married and has 5 children, manage to deposit two hundred and fifty grand in less than a year? Please tell me something. Was he selling Amway on the side? Was he skimming from the collection plate? What was it? What was he doing?"

Before Scott could answer, Senator Burke slid a large unmarked manila envelope across the table. "Take a look at this photo Scott. When you and Frances split up, this is what he did to his guide on the other side. Tell me, is this the Lord's work?"

Scott opened the envelope and pulled out two 8x10 color photographs. The pictures showed the body of a man in his 20's. His throat was cut from ear to ear, his shirt red from spilled blood. The man was clearly Afgani, Scott recognized him from the mission.

"Give me a logical explanation, Scott. By the way, in Diablo's report, he commended you for your judgment and professionalism. And believe me Scott, I personally debriefed him. He was torn up about Frances, but had to protect himself and you. God only knows what could have happened if he wasn't there."

Scott's head was spinning. He tried to think. Had Frances acted differently? Had he said anything out of character? Were there any other signs? The only mentions of money were usually professing a lack of it, but that's nothing new. Soldiers are notoriously underpaid and overworked. *It's all such a blur now. Where did the other guide go, and the rest of the villagers? Were they afraid of Frances after seeing a man killed? Impossible.*

"Scott, I am going to end this investigation now for the good of the service and all involved. Maybe there is a logical explanation, but it died 4 days ago. He's gone and that is a tragedy. But let's try to remember that he may have been his own executioner. The family will be compensated and we can all move on."

"What about me? Am I just supposed to move on? What do you have planned for me?" Scott asked.

"Scott, your record is nearly spotless. Your finances are in order. If you're dirty you're doing it for free. That's not a likely scenario. You have top evaluations from A to Z. You've got two successful SF Team commands under your belt, one in Latin America. Then you asked for another SF Team command and ended up in the Middle East. That's a good record. McCallister calls you one of the most resourceful and natural leaders in SF. Did you know that during your eighteen months in Afghanistan your team had the lowest number of firefights in the entire theater of operations?"

"No," Scott answered.

"It's true. You cleared more villages, rounded up more bad guys and established a rapport with the locals in the Afghani community. You have more quantifiable progress than any other team. And you did it with fewer bullets. In fact my sources tell me that you rarely even carried your weapon at the ready while patrolling? Why's that Scott?"

"It leaves you vulnerable, but it also makes you less threatening. Every village patrol is a negotiation. Everybody has to win. You can never impose your will on a culture. You have to…"

"…convince them that you are on their side, help them identify what they need and then help them achieve it." Burke finished the sentence for him. "McAllister's words?"

"Yes. And it's true. Storming a village with guns drawn is one technique, but just because you have a capability doesn't mean you have to use it. Sometimes it builds hatred where none existed previously."

"Here's the bottom line: your entire eighteen months in Afghanistan is classified and will remain so. I want you to listen very closely to what I am about to say. You and your team finished your entire tour in the Middle East. You returned home to Bragg to tune up on some training. Unfortunately, you wandered into a live range. Frances died trying to save the rest of the team and you were caught in the crossfire. I'm also throwing in a Silver Star for your Afghanistan service. Blaster wanted a new assignment. He's already on his way to a comfortable billet at Schoefield Barracks, Hawaii."

"What about the rest of my team?"

"They were given appropriate versions of the story. Your SF Group is about to pack up and move. They have some business to take care of in Iraq. When they rotate back stateside next year, this will all have blown over."

"So, I go down in history as the SF Captain who can't navigate, got a man killed, and myself shot?"

"You're being too hard on yourself Scott. You're going to have to get over it no matter what you decide to do," Burke said, trying to comfort Scott in a strange sort of way.

"Get over it? Move on? That's easy for you to say. Frances was a good man. It kills me to see this get pinned on his memory. This is ridiculous. Where's Diablo? Let me question him. You've done more than assign blame. You've disgraced the name of a good family. I'll move on and you can hop your flight back to D.C. and blow smoke up someone else's ass," Scott said, in an increasingly loud and insolent tone. The others in the room stopped whatever it was that they were doing, stared at Senator Burke and braced for impact.

Senator Burke's eyes grew small and dark. His facial expression remained blank as he stared through Scott's skull with an intensity that would intimidate anyone. Scott knew he had pushed too far and backtracked. "Excuse me, sir. I know you didn't make this mess. You just have to clean it up."

The color slowly returned to the senator's face. He exhaled and continued. "Name your post. You can assign yourself to any post and any position you want. You can also take as much leave as you need to get back up to speed. But remember that you are forbidden to ever discuss this incident with anybody, regardless of their clearance level."

Scott thought long and hard for several minutes while Senator Burke picked at his fingernails and commented on his need of a shoeshine. *This isn't what I signed up for.*

Two years earlier, Scott had been picked to serve on a focus group of soldiers and officers from all over Fort Bragg. Officials from the Pentagon and U.S. Army recruiting and Retention ran the one day seminar. It was not something Scott wanted to do, but he was ordered to attend.

The premise of the seminar was to provide the brass with suggestions on how they might improve morale and retention in a shrinking, post Cold War Army. Hot topics of the time were women in combat positions, gays in the military and shrinking budgets.

"I believe that standards should be adjusted to provide for more women in combat roles," offered a young female Second Lieutenant and recent West Point Graduate.

"Gays should never be allowed in the Army. They should be banned from military bases entirely," said a young, male Sergeant from Alabama.

Scott had been almost entirely quiet throughout most of the seminar and tried not to draw the attention of the Pentagon staff.

"Captain Green, would you care to comment on any of the subjects we've spoken about today?" asked the female Major in charge.

"Not really."

"Captain, please share your thoughts. We value your opinion," she replied in a cheery tone with matching fake smile.

Scott was the only SF soldier in a room full of cooks, clerks, supply personnel, infantry soldiers, communications personnel and several other specialties that he knew very little about and never interacted with. *This might ruffle some feathers but here goes.*

"Ok. As far as women in combat goes, I'm all for it. But the standards can't be touched. They exist for a reason. If the job requires a twenty mile march with a one hundred pound pack in four hours, everyone needs to meet that minimum standard."

The Major and Lieutenant made quick eye contact. The latter attempted to speak, but was cut off by the Pentagon brass. "Captain Green, don't you think women could make contributions to the Special Forces?"

"Absolutely! After they march twenty miles with a one hundred pound pack in four hours. There's a reason for that. The places where we deploy don't have a lot of convenient stores and shopping malls, so we have to carry everything we need in and out. No bell hops either.

"As for gays, I could really care less. So there you have it. That's how I feel. Can I go now?"

The Major turned red. Scott couldn't tell if she was mad or embarrassed. "No, Captain Green. You can't go now. Furthermore, you are creating a hostile environment for some of us." The Lieutenant nodded her head in agreement, her eyes squinting at Scott with rage.

"A hostile environment? How did I do that? Because my opinion differs from yours? I thought this was an open forum," Scott replied firmly, but respectfully. The male Sergeant from Alabama bounced his head in approval.

"It is, but you're not being sensitive. I would expect more from an officer of the Special Forces."

Scott could feel the blood rush to his face as he started to lose his temper. "You would? Then I guess you don't know much about SF. We're concerned with abilities and results, not sensitivity and political correctness. Now, if you'll excuse me, I have real work to do." Scott left the room and returned to his unit without another thought about the seminar.

As it turned out, the Major did know at least a little bit about SF. Her boyfriend at the Pentagon was Brigadier General Jonathan Billings, a former commander of the JFK Special Warfare Center. Scott was given a formal letter of reprimand from LTC McCallister. It was placed in his permanent file along with his latest evaluation to add some balance. He was rated above average in all categories. The letter did not hurt his career, but served as a reminder of the direction in which the military was going. Scott's tolerance for political correctness and false sensitivity would hold him back in the new army. The events of the past few days were enough. Things would never go back to being the way they were. Scott felt it was time.

"So what's it going to be?" asked Senator Burke.

"No thanks, Senator. I'm getting out. It's time to move on," Green said. He immediately felt the relief of his decision.

Burke paused for a moment, genuinely surprised. "You can't just resign Scott. You can't just walk away."

"Yes I can. My time has passed and I'm tendering my letter of resignation today."

"You've got one hell of a bright career ahead of you. You should think about this."

"I've got a little more that ten towards twenty. Should I work another decade for an already shrinking pension and slow VA healthcare? Forget it. I'm done. I'm going home."

"What's at home, Scott? No family. No home. The Army is your home. We need people like you."

"People like me? And my Team? You don't need us. You can just make more."

"Watch your tone with me. I'm a reasonable man, but don't push it."

It was time to fall on the sword. Play the game and get out.

"I apologize. I didn't mean to be disrespectful, but this is a lot for me."

Burked looked him in the eyes and waited a moment before speaking. "No problem. Perfectly understandable."

"My shoulder is killing me and I need to rest. But I'm serious about getting out. It's time to shed my skin."

"I understand completely. Maybe I can help you."

"Help me?"

"Trust me. I work for the Government," Burke said, with a grin that was charming, but obviously forced. The words echoed in Scott's head as he remembered the first time he had heard them. He and Senator Burke had met before.

Chapter 3

Norwich University
The Military College
of Vermont
12 Years Earlier

Scott pressed the snooze button on his alarm clock several times before finally rolling out of bed. Balancing cadet life with bartending at the only pub in town was not easy, but he needed the money. His shift had finally ended at 2:30AM. Three hours later it was time for Army PT (physical training). Most would choose one or the other, but Scott did both faithfully and would never complain. This was his last year of school and there was light at the end of the tunnel.

Ten minutes of stretching and calisthenics was followed by a three mile run around the hilly campus. The first few minutes were the only hard part. Soon the blood started to pump. It was a great way to start the day.

After the workout, the cadets would rush back to the barracks to shower, shave and prepare for their daily inspection and classes. At noon the entire corps would form on the upper parade ground to march down to the mess hall for lunch together. The afternoons were usually filled with more classes, sports practices and other activities. But not today, after lunch all would form back together to march to the armory for a leadership speaker. Scott had no intention of attending.

Long days of classes, late nights working at the pub and PT were taking their toll and Scott needed to get sleep whenever and wherever he could.

"Cover for me," Scott said to his Cadet First Sergeant as he left the mess hall and walked the long way around campus to avoid the formation and eyes of the commandant's assistants. Cadets were walking up the hill and starting to form on the parade ground. He had to be discreet, leadership speakers were mandatory.

The back steps to Dodge Hall were steep and there was nobody in sight. Scott decided to sprint the last few steps to get inside before anyone noticed him. At the top of the steps he bumped in Cadet Robert Wilson, his battalion commander and roommate from freshman year.

They had both chosen drastically different routes in corps life. Robert chose to follow the rules at all costs and constantly apply for cadet leadership positions. Scott chose to follow most of the rules but concentrate more on academics and being active in the Army Department. After all, they were paying his full tuition.

"You're going the wrong way Scott," said Robert.

"Actually Rob, I'm going the right way, which you happen to be in right now."

"Leadership speakers are mandatory."

"Not today. I'm exhausted and have to work again tonight. This is my only chance to grab some rack time."

"Everybody else is tired, but they're going."

"Maybe they should blow it off too. It's actually quite liberating."

"Come on Scott, don't put me in this position," Robert replied.

The position he was referring to was making the decision to look the other way or give Scott some type of disciplinary action. Leadership positions among peers are not easy, another reason Scott chose to avoid them. Cadet leaders are damned if they do, damned if they don't. Enforce the rules and you're a tool, let things slide and you're a slacker. *Besides, who wants to chase their classmates around all day enforcing petty rules? It's not like the corps is at war.*

"Well then, let me make it easy for you. Do whatever you have to do, but wait a few hours so I can rest. Bye Robert."

"Why do you do stuff like this Scott? Why can't you just play the game?"

"Robert, you need to loosen up. Go get a haircut or shine your shoes or do whatever it is that you guys do. I'm going to rack out."

Scott walked around Robert and entered through the back door. The barracks were empty, the best time to catch up on sleep.

Scott removed his boots, loosened his tie and jumped on top of his rack. It was covered by his maroon and gold Norwich blanket that hadn't been washed since his freshman year. He was asleep within minutes, taken by the rack monster. Two hours later he heard loud talking and cadets scrambling into the barracks. Scott rolled over and put his pillow over his head.

"Sirs, prepare for random inspection!" Scott heard yelled down the long, narrow hallway.

Scott stumbled to his feet and stuck his head out the door. Cadets were racing to pick up their rooms and make their beds. "What's going on?" he asked one of the sophomores who lived across the hall.

"Leadership Lab is over and the speaker is coming to walk through our barracks. They just announced it at the end of his talk."

"Who is it?"

"It was a Senator, Burke or Brick or something like that."

"I'll take my chances."

Scott returned to his rack. He was asleep again within minutes, immune to the noise. Then he heard a knock at his door as it flung open.

Scott looked up from his slumber to see a well dressed man enter his room, led by Cadet Robert Wilson. *You've got to be kidding me. What a tool you are Robert.*

"Good afternoon Sir," he said, as he rose to his feet looking completely disheveled.

"Good afternoon," replied Robert.

"I wasn't talking to you," Scott said, shooting Robert an angry look.

Senator Burke said nothing as he looked around the room. Scott's uniforms were hanging on the outside of his closet. His ties loosened enough to slip off his head and place on hangers. His boots and shoes were out or order, books and papers were scattered on his desk. The Senator shook his head and finally smiled at Scott.

"What's your name? Where are you from?"

"Cadet Scott Green, Sir. I'm from Boston."

"It's nice to meet you Cadet Green from Boston. What's your major?"

"My major is Civil Engineering, Sir."

"Is it really? That's a tough major. I was more of a liberal arts guy myself, history and English. It left me with more free time. You missed my speech didn't you?"

"Yes Sir, I'm afraid I did," Scott replied as he glared at Robert. *But you knew that didn't you Robert?*

"Well, judging from how many cadets I saw sleeping, I'd say you didn't miss much. Is that your poster?" he asked, pointing at a Special Forces poster on the wall.

"Yes Sir."

"You want to be in the SF?"

"Yes Sir."

"Good, we need good people in SF. But remember, Cadet Green from Boston, to be SF takes discipline."

"Yes Sir."

"It takes confidence and strength, all the time no matter what. Do you think you can handle that?"

"Yes Sir, no doubt," Scott replied confidently.

Senator Burke looked him up and down and smiled again. "Then you'll make it. Trust me, I work for the government." He smiled, patted Scott on the chest and swaggered out of the room. Robert was immediately on his heels.

"Thanks Robert," Scott said sarcastically.

"What are friends for? And by the way, you have five tours for missing a mandatory formation. Enjoy them. I'll be sleeping."

Chapter 4

▼

Fort Bragg Fayetteville, North Carolina

The following two months were an endless cycle of rest, physical therapy and recovery. Scott maintained a strict regimen of diet and exercise in order to shorten his recovery time so he could move on with his life. The pain medication worked pretty well and the physical therapist he was working with was exceptional. But some things you have to do on your own. His shoulder wouldn't heal correctly until he got his head on straight. The body follows the mind, not vice versa.

SF has moved around so much that even Scott found it hard to keep track of what unit is stationed where, not that it really matters. They're never home. SF Groups are constantly deployed all over the globe conducting real world missions.

The John F. Kennedy SWC (Special Warfare Center, known as "swick") had all of Scott's belongings relocated from his apartment at Ft Campbell, Kentucky to a condominium just off of Morganton Avenue in Fayetteville, NC.

Private movers did all of the work, unpacking and placing things where Scott requested. He didn't plan on being there too long, so he only unpacked the necessities and left the rest of his things in their crates and boxes. He was happy with the essentials, only needing a bed, TV, several chairs and a table. The rest was unnecessary.

Scott spent the majority of the day at the therapy center. For the few hours that he wasn't training, he stayed close to the condo. Scott preferred to read, surf on the computer and watch TV. He rarely went out, although, he still had several friends in Fayetteville. *What would I tell them? How could I explain this?*

Someone picked Scott up every morning to bring him to therapy. Not just because they were being nice, but because it made it easier for them to keep an eye on him. The car was always there in the morning waiting outside and surely someone was keeping tabs on him at all times. *What did they think I'm going to do? Brag about the mission? Tell someone? What would that accomplish?* It paled in comparison to the big stories. The country was still in collective shock, but not only because of the attack on the twin towers and fighting in the Middle East. *Surely the country would be more concerned with stories about Wall Street, terror cells, urban snipers and of course Catholic Priests.*

Scott always wondered what he'd do when he finally left the Army. Luckily he had been smart and since his very first paycheck had been putting away money to build a nest egg. He had enough money where he didn't have to worry about things for a little while, but would eventually need some source of income. Also, the Army was about to cut him a decent check for all of his hazardous duty pay, jump pay, TDY (Temporary Duty) and unused leave time. All together it would be a decent sum of money. Saving money was one of the smart things he had always done while on active duty. Then again, it's tough to blow all of your money when you're constantly being sent to the most undesirable parts of the world to deal with the most undesirable kinds of people.

Would it be any better on the other side of the fence? Who knows? At least nobody will wake me up in the middle of the night to tell me that I'm going on a six month long business trip to the middle of nowhere. It would have been ideal to have my next job lined up prior to being discharged. After I sign out for the last time I'll get into my car to head north. Then I'll play it by ear.

Green finished his last day of therapy exactly 60 days after returning from Afghanistan. He jumped off of the weight machine and wiped the sweat from his brow with a towel. The towel was new. The Special Forces logo shined bright on it. Scott decided it would make a decent souvenir and placed it in his gym bag.

"Looks like you're almost there Scott. How does everything feel?" asked Martin, Scott's physical therapist for the past 2 months.

"I feel about as good as I can without the help of chemicals. Thanks Marty, I appreciate everything."

"No problem. So, is your family excited to see you? Do you have any plans?"

"No. I don't really have a family. And my plan is to make a plan, if that makes any sense to you."

"Sure it does. Do you have a girlfriend back home?"

"No. And my job over the past few years hasn't really helped. We'll see what happens when I become a normal person again."

"Again? Something tells me you were never a normal person," Marty joked.

Scott extended his hand. "Thanks again for everything."

"No problem Scott. Good luck and be careful. I hate repeat customers," Marty said with a smile.

"I'll do my best."

Scott woke up the next morning ready to go. The same movers who helped him unpack returned to pack up his furniture and belongings the day before and the container was already on its way to a storage facility near Boston. He hadn't slept a wink all night in the empty condominium. With all of his things packed, the slightest noise reverberated throughout the entire room, reminding him of the emptiness of his life. He was left with two full suitcases. *I like it better this way, travel light.*

Scott turned his keys in to the condominium office and went directly to the administrative office at SWC. It only took a few minutes and he was out with a new sense of freedom mixed with anxiety. Scott was proud of his service to his country. In a way, he felt as though he had done his small part to help make the country and the world a better place. But he knew that he would miss his friends and was amazed at how close he had become with his fellow soldiers. When men are put in positions of great danger with little hope, they aren't fighting only for God and Country, they fight for each other, and that bond is not easily broken.

Chapter 5

Boston, Massachusetts

It was early afternoon when Scott finally hit Interstate 95 and headed north. Some people like to stop and smell the roses when they travel. Scott prefers to just get there.

He made the trip in record time. As he approached Boston from the South, the memories came flowing back. He had spent a lot of time pubbing on Thursdays, eating dinner in the North End, and being a "Bleacher Creature" for opening day at Fenway Park was a tradition. Boston is a Mecca of American history and culture. You can taste it through the scenery and atmosphere.

It was about 1:15AM, almost time for last call. Nobody was expecting him so he decided to stop in at Faneuil Hall to see Tony Denucci. Tony had been one of Scott's closest friends for almost twenty years and was a very successful restaurant owner in Boston. Actually, Denucci Corp. owns three of the hottest restaurants and bars in the city. Tony's newest venture was a place called The Revere Tavern, named after Paul Revere. Anything with a patriot theme or name usually does well with the tourists, not just congress. It was part pub and part restaurant with live music nightly. He had a tough time getting his permits in the beginning, but after he figured out exactly which city officials required compensation and which unions he needed to support, he was open and ready for business. It only took a few months and people were already considering it some kind of a historical landmark. Tourists assumed that the building had something legitimately to do with the great Paul Revere and the establishment did little to discourage the rumor. It was a Friday night and the place was packed.

Scott parked his car in one of the parking garages that would probably cost more than his bar tab and made his way towards the main entrance of The Revere Tavern. There was a line out the door with at least one hundred people in it. That meant that the bar was at its capacity of one thousand.

Scott made a promise to himself after college that his days of waiting in line to get into a bar were over. If he can't somehow accelerate his access, he'd go elsewhere or he'd go home. The main entrance had about five bouncers of various sizes regulating the flow of customers. Instead of doing the usual, asking for someone who works there by name and expecting preferential admission, he decided to have some fun.

Once Scott located the bouncer with the mechanical counter in his hand he approached him. "What's your count?" Scott asked, in a formal tone.

"Excuse me?"

"You heard me. What's the count?" Scott replied, looking him in the eyes.

"Just over a thousand, but we're thinning it out now. The band just finished and a lot of people are leaving through the back exit."

"Really?" Scott said, obviously questioning his honesty. "I'll just have to see for myself."

Scott walked past him and headed for the stairs that lead up to the main entrance. Another bouncer grabbed him by the arm from behind and tried to hold him back.

"Got a problem?" Scott asked, barely able to keep a straight face.

The first bouncer waved him off before he could respond. He gave Scott an apologetic look and returned to the door. *It's amazing how easy it is to pass yourself off as a cop. These guys are either stupid or gun shy of city officials because of all their permit problems.*

Scott made his way up the stairs and took a look around. It was full and the lines for the bathrooms extended around the corner into the lobby. He hadn't seen this many women in one place for almost two years.

It had been a long drive and Scott was thirsty. He zigged and zagged through the crowd to the main bar and tried not to look giddy in front of all the girls. He tried to order a beer. It was four people deep all the way down the line. After about three minutes someone rubbed their hand slowly across his backside. He turned around and was face to face with Angelica. Her piercing blue eyes and shiny blond hair were a welcome sight.

"Nice to see you too Scott," she said.

"Hey beautiful. Miss me?"

"Dearly. I cry myself to sleep every night," she said sarcastically.

He put his arms around her and gave her a warm hug. She hugged him tighter and kissed the side of his ear.

"How long are you in town for?" she asked.

"Don't know yet. No plans. But I'm officially a civilian now."

"Wow! I thought you liked showering with men."

"I did. But it quickly lost its luster," he replied. "Why shower with men when beautiful women like you are walking the streets alone."

"I don't exactly walk the streets, but I think I know what you mean. You gonna be around after hours?" she asked.

"Wild horses couldn't drag me away," he said, as he surveyed the crowd. He had a habit of scanning the crowd wherever he went. You could tell a lot about people by the way their gestures, their clothes, the way they carry themselves and especially the eyes. The eyes never lie.

"Still got the wandering eyes huh?"

"Negative. I'm just watching your back," he said, as he winked at her.

"I'll catch you later Schwarzkopf."

She continued navigating through the crowd holding a tray of drinks over her head, making it look easy. Angelica and Scott had flirted relentlessly since meeting about eight years previously. She was now twenty eight years old, putting herself through graduate school and working full time. They dated off and on, but with little commitment. They would come and go from each other's lives and keeping it casual made it easier for both of them.

"I hear there's some kind of building inspector here," a deep voice said from behind.

Scott turned around and Tony Denucci was standing there with a smirk on his face. Tony was tall and muscular. He never worked out but had the stamina of a horse. Scott was always impressed that they could party until the sun came up and Tony was always ready to go in the morning, having never experienced a hangover in his entire life. The restaurant and club industries chew people up and spit them out. The hours are long and the lifestyle is draining. But Tony had it in his blood. He was made for the business.

"How you doing brother?" Scott asked.

"I'm doing well. It's great to see you!"

They shook hands and gave each other an extended hug, not caring about the onlookers. The truth is that Tony was the closest thing to family that Scott had. It was Tony's family who took Scott in when his parents were killed on the night of their high school graduation, a night that Scott tried to forget and rarely spoke about.

"Let's get out of here and go someplace to talk," Tony said.

"Yes, it's time for me to see the corner office."

Tony chuckled and motioned to follow him. Instead of suffering through the crowd, they walked behind the bar and followed it for the length of the building. It was much easier. You could hear the bartenders announcing that it was last call. Buy your drink now if you need another, otherwise, get out. "You don't have to go home, but you can't stay here!" could be heard throughout the pub.

They climbed the spiral staircase in the corner of the bar and headed for Tony's office. As the door shut tightly behind them, it was instantly quiet. Tony pointed towards the door and walls. "Had to do it. The walls are soundproof. The noise drives me nuts when I'm trying to do the books."

He motioned for Scott to sit and grabbed the chair from behind his desk and moved it closer so they could toast Scott's arrival with two glasses of fourteen year old single malt scotch.

"Welcome home Scott," he said, as he raised his glass.

"Thank you, brother. It's good to be here."

They touched their glasses and both took healthy sips of Scotch. It was smooth and warm.

"Last I heard was that you were making house calls. Or should I say cave calls?"

"Yes, but not anymore. I'm officially unemployed," Scott replied.

"Any idea what you want to do?"

"Not yet. Just relax for a little while. Maybe I'll open a bar across the street from you. Either way, do you still have that spare room in your condo?" Scott asked.

"Of course, don't you still have the keys?"

"Yeah, but I just wanted to make sure."

"Don't be ridiculous. What's mine is yours, you know that. Hey, can you open that window behind you? I want to smoke, but the inspectors bust my balls big time if they smell it in the office. Why? Because it's not fair to the cleaning staff. Can you believe that? My smoke might offend people who clean toilets for a living. Unreal."

Scott chuckled and got up from his seat. He opened the window, but his shoulder was still a little stiff from the long drive and he felt a sharp pain. It must have been obvious.

"You ok?" Tony asked.

"It's nothing."

They spoke for a half hour or so about small things. All was well at home and his business was thriving. He repeatedly congratulated Scott on more than ten successful years in the military. It felt good to hear, but at the same time it made him feel worse. *Would he think the same way if he knew about my last mission and my manner of exit?*

"Well Boss, it's time for me to make my way North. It's past my bedtime," said Scott.

"No way, the night is just getting started Scott. There's a good after hours party tonight and you're my guest of honor."

"Ok. You twisted my arm."

"Cool. Go downstairs and grab a beer. I'll get my assistant manager to close up so we can get out of here. By the way, I think Angelica is coming out tonight."

The bouncers did a great job of getting the customers out beginning at the stroke of 2 AM. The place was empty except for employees by 2:10AM. It's somewhat customary for restaurant and bar workers to get together after their shifts. They don't really have much of a choice. After hours parties don't get going until 3AM or 4AM and rarely end until 8AM. Sometimes they end later. Scott was looking forward to it.

"Ready?" Angelica asked.

"Absolutely. Let's go."

They went to one of the bartender's houses. There were about a dozen people hanging out and drinking. They were all having a good time. Then Angelica asked Scott if he wanted to take a walk.

They walked down the entrance to the condominium complex and crossed the street heading towards the water. It wasn't exactly a beach, but the cool air from the Atlantic was refreshing and they were alone. Scott had been craving intimacy and Angelica spoke with a softness that he could listen to forever.

"So what the hell have you been doing? Or would you have to kill me if you told me?" she asked.

"Nothing that glamorous. Just working. You know the drill, you see the news."

"Yeah, but what was it really like?"

"It usually sucks, but sometimes you feel like you're doing some good. It's those times that make it worth it."

"Anything good war stories?"

"There's no such thing as a good war story, Angelica."

"Sorry Scott. It's just that I want to know that you were safe. It's easier for us on this end if we downplay the danger and just assume you're ok. Don't take it wrong, it's just easier for us."

"I'm safe now," Scott replied, as he looked into her eyes and raised his eyebrows.

They kissed passionately and wrapped their arms around each other. He ran his hands along the curve of her back through her Revere Tavern polo shirt. She felt soft and warm and Scott loved the smell of the pub on her.

"Hold that thought. Let's go to my apartment," she said, taking him by the hand and leading the way to his car.

They were there in less that fifteen minutes, but they couldn't keep their hands off of each other. They became more passionate and intense at every red light. It was all he could do to keep the car on the road.

"Let's get inside."

"That sounds good to me," she answered, as she bit his ear lobe and hopped out of the car.

Scott locked the car and grabbed a few items from his suitcase. She lived on the third floor and he followed her closely up the stairs from behind. He wished she had lived on the tenth floor. Her firm smooth, tan legs looked perfect in her small white shorts, he was enjoying the view.

Her apartment wasn't exactly spotless, but that's understandable considering her schedule of work and classes. The apartment consisted of one bedroom, a kitchen, one full bathroom and a decent sized family room that opened onto a small balcony. The balcony overlooked the Charles River from the Back Bay.

"Make yourself comfortable," she said, as she threw down her things and turned on the TV. "I'm going to take a shower."

Scott flipped through the channels and tried to relax. The War on Terror was everywhere. How depressing. It's obvious that the loss of lives hurts the soul of the country, but not even the terrorists could have hoped that it would consume the country this much.

Scott heard the water running in the bathroom. It was almost 4AM and he had been driving for quite some time. It was time for a shower. Angelica had just stepped in and he figured that they could save some water if he joined her.

"What took you so long?" she asked, as he wrapped his arms around her from behind. She turned around and the smile on her face quickly disappeared. She was looking directly at Scott's left shoulder.

"Oh my God Scott! What happened? What is that?"

"Just a souvenir from the past."

"That looks bad. Does it hurt?"

"Only when I laugh," he said, pressing his lips against hers.

By the time they got out of the shower and moved to the bedroom they were both overheating. They collapsed around 5:15AM and both quickly fell asleep. Scott woke up around 8AM to find a note on the night stand.

> *Scott,*
>
> *Thanks for a great night. I'm off to finish a project for school. There's coffee on the counter. Take care-Angelica*

That was it. Nothing about "give me a call", "don't go anywhere", or God forbid "I love you". Love equals loss and you can't lose what you don't have. This made things easier. Scott looked around and laughed quietly to himself as he shook his head. This is the way their relationship had always been, casual to say the least, mutually convenient at best. He couldn't recall if they had ever even had an official date. Months and even years would pass between conversations, which was the way they both liked it. No ties. No commitment. No loss.

He grabbed his things and headed for the door after drinking a cup of coffee and watching the headlines on the news channels. *Same stories, different day.* Thirty minutes later Scott was Driving north on I 93 towards Salem, New Hampshire. It was time to visit his storage area, or what he liked to call his time capsule.

Chapter 6

Salem, New Hampshire

Scott removed the key from his pocket and inserted in into the padlock. It went into the lock easily and twisted to the right, but needed a few stiff kicks before opening freely. He turned the lock sidewise and threaded it through the latch so he could remove it from the door to the storage facility. Scott bent down close to the ground and with both hands pulled the door by the handles. The rolling metal door had not been opened in two years and it took several tries to get it moving. As it broke free, Scott stood up and pushed the door high above his head with both hands. He winced as a sharp pain shot through his shoulder. *Is that ever going to go away?*

    The sunlight revealed a half full storage container with sheets over most of the contents. The air in the container was stale. Scott walked over to the left side and felt the wall for the light switch. It took a few seconds, but the overhead fluorescent bulbs eventually flickered on.

    Where do I start? The boxes were neatly stacked in the middle of the room and sat on a series of pallets to protect them from any water that might leak in. Scott removed the sheets that covered his belongings and grabbed the clipboard that sat on the top box, just as he had left it. He flipped through the inventory pages of his boxes, not quite sure what he was looking for. He was there mostly to make sure that his things were as he had left them and to move them off to the side in preparation for the arrival of his things from Fort Campbell.

Clothes, shoes and hats were in boxes one through four. Books, knick knacks and pictures were in five through nine. Box number ten was labeled "personal". There were also a few old chairs and a couch that Scott just couldn't let go. It had been the centerpiece of the rugby clubhouse at his alma mater, Norwich University, as was evidenced by the plethora of stains and the aroma of alcohol. The private military college became Scott's home and family after high school and the death of his parents. It was where he learned his first lessons about sacrifice, loyalty and brotherhood.

Scott located box number ten and took a deep breath before opening it. It was easier for him to just compartmentalize feelings and put up a wall rather than confront his emotions and experience the loss over and over again. At the top of the box was Scott's high school graduation cap. Immediately his blood began to rush and he started to sweat.

Graduating from high school is a landmark that most people never forget. For Scott it was impossible to forget, it was the night he lost both of his parents. He sat on the couch and passed the cap back and forth between his hands as he remembered the look on Tony Denucci and his parents' faces as they approached him after the ceremony.

"Hey! What a night? I can't wait until the after party," Scott said to Tony.

"Yeah, me too. Listen Scott, we have to talk with you for a minute."

"Sure, but wait. I got here early to help set up and I'm supposed to meet my parents right here. Wait until they get here so we can get a group picture."

Mrs. Denucci broke into tears and buried her head in Mr. Denucci's chest. She couldn't bear to look at Scott. Mr. Denucci nodded to Tony as he embraced his wife and slowly rubbed her back. Tony turned around to face Scott again.

"They're not coming Scott."

"No? Did they get a better offer or something?" Scott joked.

"I'm so sorry Scotty, they're not coming."

Scott looked beyond the Denuccis and saw a police sergeant talking with the vice principal who was pointing in Scott's direction. He immediately felt sick to his stomach and saliva started pouring into his mouth in anticipation of throwing up. He fought to hold back the tears and hoped to God that this was some kind of a joke.

"What…what are you talking about? They're supposed to meet me here. They're supposed to meet me here right now. The ceremony is over and we're meeting right here. They're just late, that's all," Scott wiped his eyes and stared at Tony.

"Scott. Come outside with me for a minute."

"No! No Tony! I have to meet my parents right here. I'm not moving until they get here."

"Scotty, they're not coming. Let's go outside." Tony approached Scotty and put his arm around him. Scott broke down and started to cry uncontrollably. People were watching curiously, but he didn't care. He didn't even have to hear the whole story. He knew that he had seen them that morning for the last time. His remembered his father saying goodbye as he walked out the door on his way to work. He remembered his mother kissing him gently on the cheek, hugging him and saying "I love you" as he left the house to help set up for the evening's ceremony. And he knew that those would be his last memories of them.

The investigation officially put the responsibility on the other driver, who had run a red light at an intersection only one mile from the school. He died too, which somehow made it easier for Scott. There was no one left alive to hate and blame for taking his family. But he was alone now. He had no living family to speak of. He had nothing.

The following weeks were filled with counselor after counselor. None of them were able to reach Scott in any way. He would just stare at them and occasionally smirk when they said that things would be ok. But he would listen as long as they never mentioned God. The mere mention of God or Jesus would cause Scott to stand up and walk out of the session. God was a taboo subject. No God would have allowed this to happen.

The Denucci's took Scott in for the summer and during his breaks from college. Luckily he had earned an Army scholarship and all of his expenses would be paid in exchange for service after graduation. It wasn't easy, but Scott managed to continue with life, although, forever scarred. The emotional wall had been built and never again would he let anybody get close to him. Love equals loss and you can't lose what you don't have.

The sound of a passing truck brought Scott back to his surroundings. He stood up quickly, threw his graduation cap back into box number ten and sealed it with tape. Five minutes later he had moved all of the boxes and furniture to the far side of the room so his belongings from Fort Campbell could easily fit. He gave instructions to the clerk, updated his credit card information for billing purposes and drove away, leaving his emotions behind. It made it easier for him. It was the only way he knew how to deal with the great losses in his life. And now it seemed he would have to do the same with his last mission. Just as high school culminated with the greatest loss of his life, his Army career ended with loss as well. It ended with a loss of respect, loss of control, loss of life. Where was this

God that so many people spoke of and thanked constantly? Scott knew the answer. *There is no God.*

Chapter 7

▼

Boston, Massachusetts

Tony Denucci's condominium was located in the heart of downtown Boston. It consisted of three floors with a modern gymnasium directly across the hall from the main entrance on the 4th floor. The view from the balcony off of the family room looked east over the Boston Common. When he wasn't working out or taking care of errands, Scott would sit on the balcony and think about his life. Leaving the Army was supposed to be liberating. So far, it wasn't. It only reminded him that at the end of the day he had nothing. He needed to try and keep busy, plan his next move. An idle mind is the devil's workshop.

What now? What do I do now? Look for a job? Doing what? Nothing interests me anymore. There's nothing here for me. There's nothing anywhere for me. I am officially a man without a home, without a purpose.

Scott had traveled extensively on drug interdiction operations throughout Latin America with the 7th Special Forces Group. 7th Group is responsible for 19 countries in Central and South America as well as 13 countries in the Caribbean. His SF training included intensive language instruction at the Defense Language Institute in Monterrey, California. Instructors there were continually impressed with Scott's ability to acquire not only the Spanish language, but different dialects as well. It became a game between teacher and student. The instructors would change their dialect from time to time just to see if Scott could catch on. He always did, without fail. It was the equivalent of a foreigner learning English and having the ability to travel from the Bronx to Dallas while changing their accent effortlessly. Scott was a natural. There are some things you cannot teach. Unfortunately, his proficiency in Spanish didn't help him much when his group was sent to Afghanistan to hunt terrorists. But Scott amazed his superiors and occasionally his Afghani counterparts as he became semi-conversational in Arabic after only a few weeks of self study.

The more time Scott had on his hands, the more he thought about things he didn't like thinking about. Thoughts of Diablo and SSG Frances would creep in and out of his mind. The painful memories of his parents would remind him of his loneliness. *I've got too much time on my hands and no distractions. It's time to change locations.* Scott decided to do some traveling. He had enough money put away to sustain himself for a little while and needed some time to clear his mind and make his plans for the future. There had never been any other plans except for the Special Forces. SF was his family and in the past the thought of leaving had never crossed his mind.

Diablo, who was he? Was Frances dirty? Impossible, I would have known. What would my life be like if my parents would have taken a different route to my graduation? Would I be here right now? Where would I be? Would someone else have been killed by the other car? Maybe I should have just let it go in that Afghani village. Why did Diablo have to push my buttons? Why didn't I just keep walking when I saw the corral? I'd be back with my team right now, my family. I have too many questions and not enough answers.

Scott stood up and went to the kitchen. He was shaking from too much thinking. His heart pounded and he was sweating. It felt like one of the panic attacks he used to experience shortly after his parents' accident. He removed a tall glass from the cabinet and filled it almost to the top with Jack Daniels. He added a splash of Coca Cola and finished the whole thing in one gulp. He lifted his head towards the ceiling, closed his eyes and took a deep breath. The booze was warm and he exhaled slowly as the warmth traveled through his extremities. It had been a long time since he had done that. It felt good, too good.

Scott heard the front door open and Tony walked in with a bag of groceries. Scott rinsed out the glass and placed it in the sink. Then he turned and looked down from the balcony to the entrance.

"Hey," he said casually.

"Hey. What's happening?"

"Nothing, just relaxing. Need some help?"

"Nope. It's just a few things for tonight. I have the night off and I have a dinner guest coming over at around 8 O'clock, which gives me exactly one hour to transform this bachelor pad into my little Shangri La of love. I will be preparing my specialty."

"What's that?"

"I'm not quite sure yet, but I think I'll throw all this stuff into the Wok and call it a stir fry. Care to join us?"

"No thanks. I have no desire to be the third wheel, besides I'd feel terrible if she ignored you the whole night and hung on my every word."

"Not bloody likely," Tony said, in a very bad cockney accent.

"Besides, I was just about to head out. Leave a light on for me," Scott said, as he grabbed his keys from the kitchen table and passed Tony on the stairs.

"Whew! How's the Jack treating you?" Tony said, as he waved his hand in front of his nose. Scott ignored him and closed the door behind him.

It was a cool night in Boston as Scott walked around Faneuil Hall. Tourists and locals mingled as they walked the cobblestone streets, stopping occasionally to watch the street performers. After completing two laps of the open air marketplace, he sat on a bench and decided that he wouldn't get up until he knew where he was going to travel. Jamaica was an option, but it's too touristy. Cuba would be cool but Americans can't travel there without permission. Scott had never been too concerned with rules, but why risk it?

What about Central America? Too many revolutionary groups that could ruin your day. South America is an option. But there are a lot of problems down there too. Where can I go to just chill out and think? Where can I relax and exist in relative anonymity? Where can I find cold beer and warm weather?

As Scott pondered his destination he watched as two beautiful young women walked through the marketplace together, talking quietly and smiling. They both wore low cut jeans and small t-shirts that exposed their bellies. Surprisingly, neither of them had a naval piercing. As they got closer Scott heard them conversing in Spanish. They were speaking about nothing in particular, which is usually the case with young Latin Americans. He was always amazed at their uncanny ability to sit and talk for hours about absolutely nothing.

Scott smiled at them and was happy when they returned his smile. One grabbed the other by the arm and pulled her towards Scott. He heard her say to the other. "Ask this guy."

"Excuse me. Do you know what time it is?" She asked in English.

Without looking at his watch, Scott replied in Spanish. "It's almost nine o'clock."

The girls looked at each other and smiled. "Oh, you speak Spanish."

"A little," Scott lied.

"Thank you," said the first girl, as they turned to continue their walk.

Scott thought to himself and called out to them. "Hey. Where are you ladies from?"

"Cambridge."

"No. I mean originally. Where are you from originally?"

"La República Dominicana," one of the girls said over her shoulder, as she continued to stroll slowly, arm in arm with her friend. He loved the way it rolled off of her tongue.

Ladies and gentlemen we have a verdict. Next stop: the Dominican Republic.

Chapter 8

Santo Domingo
Dominican Republic

Scott returned to the condominium immediately. Tony's dinner must have gone well because he and his date were nowhere to be seen. Scott walked up the stairs to the loft and turned on the computer. It was research and planning time. Websites and message boards about the Dominican Republic were easy to find.

One of the first things Scott learned was that the Dominican Republic is otherwise known as "the DR", not "the Dominican". Referring to it as "the Dominican" will drive most people in the know crazy. That would be like calling New York "the New". *That's good to know.*

Christopher Columbus landed in Santo Domingo during his second voyage. *I wonder what he was actually looking for. Or was he just like me? Maybe Chris didn't have anything at home either. Too bad I couldn't get someone to finance my voyage like Chris did. What a lucky man.*

Scott surfed through the internet and found more information than he needed. He was able to locate several small family run hotels and put together an itinerary in his head. Small hotels were always the way to go if you wanted to blend in. Big resorts are an expensive waste of time and they shield visitors from the real society. This was not so much a vacation, but an informal escape into a different culture.

Scott made all of the proper arrangements for his things in Boston. Six days later he stepped off the plane and immediately felt the sweat start to build all over his body. It was similar to other places he had visited, but the smell was different. No bad, just different. Every place has its own distinctive smell and Scott had experienced many.

The baggage carousel was packed with Dominicans returning from the U.S. to visit their families. Each had a different story about their experiences in the land of opportunity. Some thrived and some withered. Scott was always taught that the U.S. was indeed the land of opportunity, but there are no guarantees. Sink or swim. Fish or cut bait. At the end of the day it's up to individuals to make it happen.

Immigration was a popular discussion topic in the officer's club. LTC McCallister would always sum it up with one comment. "There's got to be a reason that people from all over the world want to live in the U.S. so badly that they will strap themselves to flimsy rafts and try to paddle their way." Scott agreed.

Waiting for luggage can be painful so Scott carried on. This made things faster and easier when traveling and also made him only pack the essentials. Others cramped together while mindlessly watching a parade of cheap looking bags and suitcases. Scott always thought it was fun to pick a bag and try to predict who will grab it. You can tell a lot about someone by their bags.

Scott walked right by the luggage zombies with his bags and was one of the first in line at Immigration. The agent didn't even look up at him as he stamped Scott's passport and motioned to keep walking towards Customs.

Customs was the same drill. They paid more attention to the returning Dominicans than any of the tourists on board. Within a few minutes Scott was rolling his suitcase behind him as the automatic doors opened up revealing an ocean of people waiting behind giant crowd barricades. *All of this for me?* Scott thought as he walked through the doors.

"Taxi! Taxi!"

"Hello, my friend! Where you from?"

"Americano! Americano! I help you. How much money you has?"

After expressing no interest and generally ignoring all of the men as they argued over who would get to drive him, Scott negotiated a price with a respectable looking young man and was off towards Santo Domingo.

"I'm Carlos. What you name friend?" he asked.

"Scott."

"Where you from?"

"Boston."

"Pedro Martinez! He is from the town over there!" he said, as he pointed in the direction of San Pedro De Macoris.

"Actually, he's from Santo Domingo. You're thinking of Sammy Sosa."

"Oooohhhh Damn! You right! You right!"

"Why you here friend? Vacation? For the girls? What you need, I help you get it?"

Scott replied in Spanish. "I need a ride to my hotel. Nothing more."

"Ah, you speak Spanish. Ok, no problem. I'll get you there."

The cab turned west towards Santo Domingo. The roads were in poor condition all over the country, but the Dominicans don't seem to mind. They drive with a sense of extreme urgency and occasional outright insanity. Scott watched as the sun reflected off the turquoise water. He had seen many sunsets inland, but preferred to witness them seaside. Nothing compared to the tranquility of watching the yellow sun become orange as it appeared to plunge into the water. Peaceful darkness would soon follow.

After a short series of twists and turns they were on the main strip and within striking distance of Scott's hotel. All of the major hotels were along the water, but Scott decided on a small family run hotel two blocks north, named simply, La Casa de la Familia.

The small, two storied hotel had a small driveway with only four or five parking spaces in front. Scott got out of the car and grabbed his bags from the back seat. He had negotiated a fare of three hundred pesos at the airport. Scott handed the driver a crisp five hundred Peso bill then placed his bags on the curb. He heard a loud "Thank you!" and turned around just in time to see Carlos drive away without offering Scott his change. Scott shook his head and laughed to himself. *Lesson learned.*

He was greeted at the desk by an older woman with a beautiful and genuine smile. Although there was nobody else in the registration area, it still took about twenty minutes to get checked in. *Slow down honey, there's no need to rush.*

Scott went to his room, immediately cranked up the air conditioning and turned on the TV so he could listen to the news while he unpacked. After about two minutes he changed the channel to the music station. The news was always the same.

The bathroom was decent size for a small hotel. Scott hopped in the shower and relaxed for a good twenty minutes. His shoulder was stiff from not moving it much on the plane and the hot water felt good on it. At least it did for the first few minutes before the temperature changed to freezing cold.

Scott climbed out of the shower and wrapped a towel around himself. He felt like a new man. The air conditioner had cooled the room down in spite of the electricity constantly coming and going, alternating between the main line and the generator on the roof. He had read about the electricity problems prior to arriving, but didn't imagine that when people said it went out a lot, they meant as constantly as this. *Thank God for the generator. Actually, thank the lady downstairs. God has nothing to do with it.*

After unpacking entirely and relaxing for an hour or so, Scott decided to do some exploring. Where better to start than the Colonial Zone? Columbus went there first too. He got dressed and emerged from the hotel wearing loose linen pants and a black shirt. There was a man standing next to a beat up car in front of the hotel.

"Taxi Senor?"

"No gracias."

Most books about Latin America recommend against walking alone at night. But those books are directed at the casual tourist. Scott is a professional. He speaks the language, but that's the easy part. Communication is predominantly physiological and psychological, not linguistic. It's all about the way you walk, stand, think and exist. It would only take Scott about an hour to adapt to the environment and blend as much as possible.

Americans generally walk fast, talk fast and look paranoid when in different environments. Scott doesn't. He walks slowly, like he knows where he's going and he's been there a million times. He speaks slowly and confidently. He makes eye contact when he should and casually looks away when he shouldn't. He almost never crosses the street when walking towards a group of people to avoid them. And he never shows a hint of weakness or strength. He looks like he belongs there. In Latin America there are times when you should keep a low profile and there are times when you should stick your chest out and be macho. The challenge is identifying when to do which.

Scott passed by the many statues and monuments that decorate the ocean side and found himself in the Colonial Zone in about twenty five minutes. The walk was uneventful, but informative. The streets were filled with people. The musical beats of Merengue and Bachata could be heard everywhere, sometimes at an ear piercing volume. Families congregated outside their homes on plastic chairs, drinking rum, Presidente beer and playing dominoes. Dominican communities are extensions of the family and everyone knows everyone else's business.

All are welcome and expected to wander from home to home in search of conversation and the latest news. Who is marrying who? Who is working where? And of course, who is doing something that they shouldn't be doing. To walk through the neighborhood without socializing would be rude, time being free. Neighbors also serve as a support network for those in need. Most neighbors become unofficial cousins, aunts and uncles, extensions of the immediate family. It is a familial atmosphere which is almost absent in the United States.

The Colonial Zone is much different than the rest of Santo Domingo. The buildings are circa 1500, the streets are narrow, and the atmosphere is festive. Colors burst around every corner. Bright red next to yellow and green distract from the rough cobblestone streets. It is a conglomeration of colors unseen outside of the Caribbean.

There are very few modern buildings. The streets are filled with tourists, outnumbered by legions of street hustlers masquerading as legitimate tour guides. Scott strolled along and watched.

He ignored everyone who tried to speak with him, no matter how nice they tried to appear, now was not the time. The pleasantries are usually just the tip of the hook that would get you into some kind of undesirable situation.

He continued to walk until he reached the Columbus Cathedral, stopping to observe the thirty foot high statue of the famous explorer. The figure of Columbus stands tall with a navigation compass in one hand, his other arm outstretched and pointing to something in the distance.

What were you actually looking for Chris? Did you find it? Or were you running from something? And did you get away? You can't run from yourself, even I know that. You can get some space, but eventually we always catch up to ourselves.

Scott looked around and decided to start the walk back towards the hotel. There was no rush, no timeline, and no mission. Most people would love it, but it made Scott itch. Keeping busy is the only way to avoid the ghosts of the past.

He stopped several times at the corner stores on the way back to buy drinks. But he was always careful to moderate his intake. Some drink alcohol to escape their emotions. Scott was the opposite, keeping control of his faculties helped him keep the bricks of his emotional wall intact.

Chapter 9

▼

Terrorist Tracking Center (TTC) Richmond, Virginia

Steven Barnes, the supervisor of the TTC, had always been known for his intense and dramatic reactions to pressure. Today was no different. He tried to push the door open before the sensor could register his palm print and optical scan, resulting in further delay. He took a deep breath, stepped back from the door allowing it to reset and slowly advanced again. This time he was patient and waited the three to five seconds required for verification. When the light turned green, he entered and was advancing towards his senior technician before the door shut tightly behind him.

"This is hot Smitty," he said quickly, as he walked past a dozen or so men and women sitting in front of large banks of computers and other machines that he knew almost nothing about.

"Everything's hot," Smitty replied. *Why does he always come to me?*

"Stop being a wiseass, this one is hot, hand delivered to me by Senator Burke himself."

"Hand delivered huh? Wouldn't that mean that he delivered it to you? Or do you mean he "hand delivered" it to you after blowing his dog whistle and you came a runnin?" Smitty said, amused with his own humor.

"Smitty, I'm going to pretend that I didn't hear that. But take this as a warning: your attitude and surly comments are melting the ice under your feet. You're here because of your skills and technical expertise. If you had to actually deal with people this center would have been shut down before we started. Lighten up and maybe I'll remember you when I'm Deputy Director of Homeland Security."

Smitty nodded his head unconvincingly without speaking and slowly spun his seat around to face the boss.

"What can Smitty's house of knowledge do for you today, Chief?"

Barnes placed his briefcase on the desk next to Smitty's workstation and opened it with both thumbs. He removed a thick file and handed it to him.

"This is a first for us. He's American, but he's also an ex operator."

Smitty opened the file and whistled as he looked at the official Department of Defense photo stapled to the inside flap. He thumbed through the file quickly, reading highlights and noting interesting sections that he would have to analyze more closely later.

"He's an SF officer. This is certainly a first. Why are we tracking this guy? Did he convert? Change his name to Abdul or something?"

"That's not your concern. Just set him up in the system and track him, Level One Red."

"One Red huh? Nice. That puts him in the top tier."

"Just find him and track him, that's what you do right? I want to know where he is and what he's doing at all times. No mistakes on this one, your career might be riding on it."

"You mean yours primarily and mine by default?"

"Just do it. His last known location was Boston, but he traveled to the Dominican a few days ago, no return ticket. He could be in and out or he may be there to stay. Don't rule anything out."

"You mean the Dominican Republic?"

"That's what I said."

"No, you said the Dominican."

"Where the hell else would I mean?"

"Ok, whatever. I get it. Any restrictions?"

"None. Track it all, emails, banking, phone calls, everything. Use any and all resources, above or under the table."

"Ok. Got a codename for him?"

"Yeah, let's go with....ah.....what do you call people who live outside of their native country?"

"They're called expatriates."

"Perfect." Barnes said, as he scribbled the letters X-P-A-T-R-I-O-T on the outside of the file.

"No. It's spelled E-X-P-A-T-R-I-A-T-E."

"Whatever. Since we don't know anything about what this guy is doing yet, let's go with the X factor. He might have been a patriot before, but now he's probably not. Call him Xpatriot."

"You mean he might not be a patriot. We're just tracking him right? He hasn't actually done anything wrong," Smitty offered.

"He wouldn't have been given to me if he was clean. Call him Xpatriot."

"It's grammatically incorrect, but you're the boss," Smitty said, as he spun his chair back around and went to work.

Barnes lingered for a few moments before exiting. As he exited, Smitty picked up the file and a green felt tipped pen. He circled Barnes' writing and neatly wrote below it in large block letters: AKA Scott Green.

Chapter 10

Santo Domingo
Dominican Republic

Mornings in the Caribbean are typically quiet. This one was no exception. Scott opened his eyes and relaxed in bed for about five minutes before slowly sitting up, draping his legs over the side of the bed and standing. He stretched his arms above his head, winced at his shoulder pain and walked to the mini refrigerator for some water. After guzzling the remainder of the bottle, he turned on the radio and began to stretch. He felt surprisingly limber until he got to his shoulder muscles. It took him another five minutes until he felt warm enough to run.

Scott slipped on a t-shirt and shorts, and laced up his running shoes. He locked the door behind him and placed the key into the inside pocket of his shorts. The sweat was beginning to accumulate before he exited the hotel.

After smiling at the desk clerk, he headed out the door and started running towards the water. After two blocks he turned left and ran parallel to the blue water of the Caribbean. The air was fresh and the streets were relatively empty. Randomly, the water would crash against the seaside rocks and spray onto the sidewalk, providing a short, but refreshing spray to passers by.

Scott never liked running, but understood the benefits nonetheless. Get the blood pumping, endorphins swirling, sweat out the toxins and clear your mind. If he went two or three days without exercising, he could tell immediately. He'd then reach for his shoes and hit the road. He never ran at a fast pace, but steady and strong. Running became his meditation and time for deep contemplation.

Diablo. Frances. What did I miss in Afghanistan? What did they tell McCallister about me? There has to be another piece to this puzzle. Frances was a good man. Who are you Diablo? Where are you now?

Scott paused to run in place as he waited for the traffic light to change. There were several semi-official looking men dressed in gray uniforms with big white safari hats. They were unarmed. Over the course of the next 3 miles he noticed similar men at a number of different intersections. *What are these guys waiting for?*

His question was soon answered as he approached a major intersection on his way back to the hotel. Two of the men entered the intersection, stopped all traffic and waited. They held portable radios to their ears as they stood emotionless. Horns and screams soon followed as the angry commuters sat and waited for what appeared to be nothing.

Two minutes later a caravan of large SUV's with police escorts rapidly approached the intersection traveling in the left lane, swerved around the other cars and made a sharp left turn, continuing on their way. Scott shrugged. *What was that all about?*

"Sir, was that someone important?" he asked the nearest white hat who had returned to the sidewalk and waved the traffic through.

"It's the Vice President or maybe the President" he replied, without looking to see who was asking.

"Gracias."

"Siempre."

Scott waited for a gap in the now increasing traffic and crossed the street. He estimated the hotel to be a half mile from the intersection and decided to pick up the pace for the final push home. Feeling surprisingly strong, he pushed it even more until his shoulder began to throb. The pounding of his feet reverberated up and throughout his entire left arm, the epicenter of pain being in the front and back of his deltoid. He thought he could actually feel his pulse around the entry and exit points of Diablo's bullet. *Thanks for the souvenir Diablo. I wish I could have given you something.*

Scott retrieved the key out of his shorts and unlocked his door, glancing to the left and right before opening it and entering. It was a force of habit to always be aware of his surroundings. He locked the door behind him, grabbed another bottle of cold water and sat on the floor to stretch. After twenty minutes of various stretching exercises and a few pushups and crunches, he peeled off his clothes and headed for the shower.

The cold water was refreshing and he continued to drink from the bottled water that he brought into the shower with him. He finished the bottle, held back the shower curtain and tossed it into the trash can under the sink. *Two points! The crowd goes wild!*

After toweling off he reached for his razor, sprayed some shaving cream into his hand and looked at himself in the mirror. He felt and looked different. The scar on his shoulder was getting better, but would be with him for the rest of his life, a painful reminder of his last days of service.

Scott decided not to shave, turned on the water and washed the shaving cream out of his hand. *Maybe it's time for a new look. Let's see how the beard looks after a few more days.*

He wrapped the towel around his waist and sat in the chair next to the window. He closed his eyes to breathe deeply, slow down his heart rate, and reflect. Most people welcomed thoughts and emotions during their meditation. Scott didn't. He used his quiet time to reinforce the emotional wall that he built the day he lost his parents. Nothing could penetrate it, everything bounced off. Creeping thoughts about purpose, meaning, love and God were quickly dispensed with. Letting emotions wander freely can make you weak and vulnerable. Love equals loss. And you can't lose something you don't have.

Scott had always looked at relationships as a potential for loss, never as a potential for happiness. But there was a part of him, deep down where he rarely looked, that wished it were different. There was a part of him that knew you could not gain without risk. He had never been in love in any of his relationships. He never let it get that far. The wall was impenetrable. But as long as that small part of him knew that he would never be complete without love and a deeper meaning, there was still hope. He would never acknowledge it, but he hoped that things would one day change.

Chapter 11

Colonial Zone
Santo Domingo

The internet café on El Conde Street was more like a sauna. Scott sat in front of the computer with a small fan blowing on his face from six inches away. It wasn't the most comfortable place in the world, but the connection was fast and he was able to check his email and surf around quickly. He finished reading his weekly newsletters, logged off the computer and gave fifty pesos to the pretty young woman at the register.

"Gracias."

"Adios."

Scott had managed to see the historical sites that interested him all before noon. Now that he was finished in the cafe, it was time for a bite to eat. He strolled down the street, keeping close to the buildings that provided shade and brief escapes from the blistering sun.

The street was again full of tourists and the shops were bustling. Voices got louder as negotiations became more intense. Tourists would cower and reluctantly agree on the shopkeeper's prices so as not to offend them. The shopkeepers would take the money, sell their products and laugh after the tourists departed. Dominicans are great actors. Scott would watch as they would wave their arms, testify to the quality of their products and feign genuine insult. The show could be seen all day.

Café Los Ojos is positioned roughly in the middle of the busy walkway and seemed the best place from which Scott could watch people and eat lunch. The open air café was half full, but that didn't seem to bother the seven or eight waitresses who gathered near the bar to talk and pass the time, occasionally waiting on customers. Dominicans have the ability to talk on and on for hours about nothing particularly important. Contrary to popular belief the national sport is gossip, not baseball.

When Scott entered, they turned and smiled at him, then quickly resumed their conversation. He chose a table just inside the door and out of the sunlight, but with a good view of the street. After five minutes he turned around towards the waitresses and waved. *The food better be good and the beer cold. I doubt people come here for the service.*

Forty five minutes and two beers later he paid the check and went on his way. The girls turned from their conversations to smile as he exited with a casual wave and an "Adios".

It was hotter than before and Scott could feel the effect of the two beers in his legs. He stopped at a kiosk and bought a bottle of cold water and started to drink from it as the man next to him spoke.

"Hey Americano. Where you from?"

"Canada," Scott replied without looking.

"My brother has a place I think you would like. He has everything. Not too far from here too. I could bring you there."

A place you think I'd enjoy? Based on what, your wealth of knowledge of me?

"No thanks. I have everything I need."

"Ok, but take this," he handed a business card to Scott and continued. "My name is on the back. Make sure you tell him you're a friend of mine and he'll take care of you like a V.I.P.!"

"Sure. Thanks."

The card read *Club de Los Reyes*, the club of kings. And then in bad English: *For all of your nightclub needs, V.I.P. lounged, air cool, class.*

"It sounds charming," Scott said, as he put the card in his back pocket and continued walking down the street. It was still early afternoon and he decided to return to the hotel and check out the pool. But first, he walked to the end of the street to see the Columbus Statue again.

There were always people around the statue and cathedral, taking pictures, looking, reading the plaque. Some would sit for hours on the benches that encased the plaza, watching the pigeons and tourists as they paced back and forth, pecking and taking pictures. Scott sat down on an empty bench and watched the people pass before hailing a taxi for a ride back to the hotel.

Thirty minutes later he emerged from his room wearing his swimming trunks, flip flops, sunglasses and a towel flung over his shoulder. He descended the back stairs and asked the woman at the front desk where the pool was.

"Arriba, on the roof."

"Gracias."

Scott was sweating profusely as he reached the top of the stairs and opened the door to the roof. There were five or six beach type chairs on the left and to the right was an above ground pool. It was slightly larger than a kiddie pool.

Is this an above ground or above roof pool? Maybe the assembly directions didn't translate well. But it's all mine today!

After removing his flip flops and applying sunscreen, Scott leaped over the edge and into the pool, eager for some relief from the heat. The water was warm but still cooler that the air and it felt good. He swam back and forth and then relaxed as he reclined back against the wall. *Ah, the good life. Maybe I'll check out the King's Club tonight. My schedule seems to be clear.*

Chapter 12

▼

Colonial Zone
Santo Domingo

The taxi driver knew exactly where to go when Scott mentioned the King's Club. They sped away from the hotel and raced towards the colonial zone, arriving in less than ten minutes. Scott paid the driver, exited the car and stepped onto the curb to look up at the sign. It was small and almost unnoticeable, the kind of place you had to be looking for to find.

Before he could push open the door, it swung open and a tuxedoed man with only one front tooth smiled widely and waved him in.

"Gracias."

"Welcome, my friend," he replied in broken English. "Many pretty ladies here at night."

A long, narrow hallway connected the entrance to the main club. It was large, dark and had a mahogany bar that stretched the length of the far wall. Scott approached and sat at an empty seat. There were very few people. *Maybe it's early.*

The bartender approached and slapped his hand on the bar loudly.

"What can I get you my friend?"

"I'll take a beer, the coldest one you have."

"They're all cold, my brother," he said, as he reached into the cooler and popped off the cap of a near frozen beer. The green bottle was covered with a thin white frost that he proudly displayed to Scott like a bottle of fine wine. "That cold enough for you?" he asked rhetorically before wrapping a napkin around the base and handing it to Scott.

"Yes it is."

"How did you find us?"

"I bumped into this guy today," Scott said, as he removed the business card from his shirt pocket and tossed it onto the bar.

The man looked at the back of the card and laughed. "My brother owes me money, which he don't got. So I tell him to send me people, which he don't know. You're the first in weeks, but I can't be mad. Hey, he's blood right?"

"I guess so."

Scott sat back and exhaled. "So where is everybody?"

"It's a late crowd in Santo Domingo, brother. We don't close 'til 5AM so people don't go out 'til midnight sometimes. But this place jumps. There'll be plenty of girls and booze later. You see one you like just let me know and I'll make it happen for you."

"Make it happen for me huh?"

"Yeah man. They do what I say or I don't let them in. Besides, a gringo with money is an easy sell."

"In that case, I'm sure I can handle it myself. But thanks for the offer."

"Whatever you want, brother."

Scott finished his beer and motioned for another one. While the bartender pulled it out of the cooler, Scott read the plaque above the cash register. It read: *Jesus is watching*.

"What's with the plaque? You don't strike me as the religious type."

"Religious? No man. That's Jesus up there, bro," he said, as he pointed to the balcony above the dance floor.

Jesus was his security man, who watched over the club, its patrons, employees and most importantly the cash register. He stood in the overwatch position with his arms crossed in front of his chest. He smiled and nodded at Scott as the bartender pointed. He was one of the biggest men Scott had seen in a long time, with short hair and big eyes.

Scott stayed at the club for a few hours watching baseball on the television. People began to arrive and Scott was soon reminded why his nightclub days were behind him. The majority of the people were trying too hard to be someone they were not. Every woman was a runway model, every man rich. There was little genuine human interaction, it was a show and Scott had no tolerance for plastic people.

Scott was tired. He paid his bill, stood up from his seat and walked out of the club. A line of taxis were waiting along the street, all competing for the fare. Scott ignored them all, walked to the front of the line of cars and entered the first one. The driver quickly ran around to the driver's side, jumped in and started the car.

He was soon back in his room with the air conditioning turned on, laying on the bed drinking a bottle of water and thinking. It had only been two days, but it was time to switch locations already, he had too much time to think and needed to continually distract himself. A change of scenery would do just that. Scott opened the phone book and flipped to the car rental agencies. *It's time to see the rest of the island.*

Chapter 13

North Coast Dominican Republic

The phone rang at 9AM as Scott finished packing his suitcase and duffel bag. The rental car representative was waiting at the front desk. He was sure that he had everything in his bags, but made one last sweep through the room, looking under the bed and opening each drawer of the dresser. It was a habit instilled in him by his mother during the few vacations they took as he was growing up. It made him remember her soft kiss on his cheek the last time he saw her alive. It was a kiss forever burned into his memory. Then he blocked it out, locked the door behind him and walked down the stairs to the front desk.

"Everything was ok?"

"Yes. Everything was fine thanks."

"Are you ever coming back?"

"I might come back, but today I'm heading for the north coast."

"It's very beautiful there. I have family in Puerta Plata."

"Great, I'll keep an eye out for people who look like you," Scott said. He then winked at her before picking up his bags and leaving.

Scott paid the rental car representative, pulled out of the driveway and started driving north. He had to turn back and forth a few times before he could get to the two lane highway, but eventually he was out of the city and on his way. His t-shirt was sticking to him so he unrolled all of the windows to let the air in.

Scott was happy to see Santo Domingo as it got smaller in his rear view mirror. There was too much concrete. He needed a good dose of nature to calm his anxiety and distract him from thinking too much. Whenever he allowed his mind to wander, he didn't like where it ended up. If allowed to wander unchecked, his conscience would turn back on himself to look for meaning, significance, some resemblance of a plan.

The military, more especially the Special Forces, were a remedy for him. It had kept him busy, focused, and constantly moving. But now, for what seemed like the first time in his adult life, he felt like he was running in place, treading water. *What the hell am I supposed to do now?*

The SF motto, "De Oppresso Liber", liberate the oppressed, had given him significance. He felt that every single mission had historical significance. Many of the missions were publicized, but most were not and never would be. But that didn't take away from his contributions. SF troops rarely perform their duties for the glory. Recognition was for the weak and egotistical. Scott always felt a calling to help those who couldn't help themselves. Whether it was in uniform or not, that was what he needed to do to survive, to have significance. But he felt himself slipping. His pride and feelings of importance were slipping away more everyday. *What now? I fell like it's all over. No mission.*

After two hours of driving with no radio or other interruptions, Scott pulled the car over to a small roadside café. His hands were trembling a bit and his heart rate was accelerated. *What's happening to me?*

He ordered a small bottle of Brugal rum, a small cup of ice and a plastic bottle of Coke. As soon as the waitress placed the items on the table, he grabbed them without looking up, mixed a strong drink and gulped it down. She stood next to the table staring at him with a blank expression. After shaking his head and exhaling, he looked up and said "Gracias." She turned and walked away without changing her expression and returned to her stool at the end of the bar.

Why am I doing this? I don't even like to drink. I just need something to calm me down. It's just a phase, that'll go away. I just need to keep moving. Stop thinking. Stop.

Scott asked for another cup of ice, got back into the car and kept driving. He hoped it wouldn't happen again. But if it did, he was prepared.

Scott let the car coast down the mountain as he descended the final approach to the north coast. He quickly came to the realization that this was the most beautiful part of the island. It appeared to be cleaner, more spacious and the temperature was a bit cooler than the capital. Puerta Plata is a major tourist destination and Scott would have plenty of resort choices. He decided to ride along the water until one caught his eye.

La Casona Dorada was the first resort sign to keep his attention so he turned left and entered the parking lot. He parked in the first available space, grabbed his bags and walked into the open air reception area.

"Hello sir. Do you have a reservation?"

"No. Do you have anything available?"

"As a matter of fact we have had a few cancellations. You are lucky."

Scott turned and looked at the empty lobby and could see out the back to the pool area. There were only six or seven people bathing in the sun.

"Yeah, you guys look busy."

Scott took his key and walked across the lobby to the elevator. He was followed by the oldest bellboy he had ever seen. *Man, this guy has got to be seventy years old.*

Scott tried to relieve the man of one of the bags after they entered the elevator, but he refused. When they reached the room the man pulled the key from Scott's hand and insisted on opening the door himself. Scott obliged and took a step back.

They entered the room and Scott immediately walked towards the window and turned the air conditioning on full blast. The old man placed his bags on the bed, stood by the door and ceremoniously put out his hand. Scott placed a modest tip into the old man's hand. He left without saying thank you. *Oh well, if I was carrying bags at his age I'd be bitter too.*

Scott unpacked his clothes, changed into his trunks and arrived at the pool within ten minutes of check in. The water was cool, much cooler than the rooftop pool in Santo Domingo. There were several employees whose sole jobs were to ensure the comfort of the guests. In spite of this, they sat amongst themselves at the end of the bar. If guests wanted service they had to approach and inquire. The employees would then look at each other until one of them would get up and see to the needs of the guest. Scott leaned against the wall in the shallow end of the pool and watched. *I think I know why labor is so cheap here.*

Scott swam to the deep end and climbed up the ladder. He decided against asking for service and instead retrieved two towels from the main cabana and chose a reclining seat at the far end of the pool. He purposely chose the far end of the pool so as to be far away from the other guests and their children. It didn't help. He closed his eyes and heard a small voice just as he was drifting off to sleep.

"What happened?"

Scott opened his eyes and saw a young boy of about ten standing in front of him. "Excuse me?"

"Your shoulder, what happened?"

"Well, I had an accident."

"What kind of accident?"

"It was a bad accident."

"Did anyone die?"

Scott was speechless. What could he say? *Yeah kid, as a matter of fact someone did die. Now get lost.*

"Well, actually…"

"Francisco. Francisco. Please come here right now. I'm sorry. He's a friendly boy," said a young woman as she approached.

"That's ok. It's no problem."

"I told him not to bother anyone, but he is so curious that sometimes he…" she hesitated as she noticed Scott's scar. "Sometimes it gets the best of him."

"Don't worry about it. He seems like a nice kid."

She smiled again, grabbed Francisco by the hand and walked back towards their section of the pool. As they walked, Francisco turned around and waived to Scott. Scott smiled and waived back.

The rest of the afternoon was spent relaxing poolside. Scott's interaction with Francisco had put a smile on his face. He read a copy of the local newspaper and the activities schedule of the resort. Scott was never one for such events, but it was fun to read about. Cocktail hour, volleyball games, free windsurfing lessons and other events were scheduled daily. *No thanks, I'm just fine doing my own thing.*

It was near the end of the day as Scott sat watching the others at the pool gather their things so they could return to their rooms and prepare for the dinner buffet. He watched as employees who had been otherwise absent during the day flocked to help them gather their things and collect the towels. They smiled as they held out their hands for tips.

Francisco's mom dressed him in his t-shirt and sandals and towel dried his hair. When she was finished, she combed it with her hands and kissed him lightly on the cheek before telling him to stay with his father as she tended to other needs. Scott felt like he had been struck by lightning. The gentle kiss on the cheek brought him back to the day that changed his whole life. Scott's mother had kissed him the same way the last time he saw her. He had been older than Francisco, but the casual situation was the same. It was a typical goodbye, not forever, but just for the moment, just as Scott's had been.

Panic set in. Scott felt his heartbeat soar and began sweating profusely. *What the hell is my problem? I dealt with this and moved on years ago. Didn't I? Forget it, block it out. Block it out. Let it pass.*

Scott got up from his seat and walked directly to the bar. The employees sitting at the end saw him approach and stared blankly at him for several minutes.

"Are one of you going to help me? Or are you just going to sit there?"

After no reply or visible evidence of action, Scott reached over the bar for a bottle of rum, gave a mock salute to the group and shouted out his room number. "Charge it to room two forty and don't get up."

He turned, slipped on his flip flops and started heading for his room. He felt numb all over, tingling and numb. The sweat poured down his face and chest.

"Sir! Sir! Please wait, sir!"

Scott ignored the man behind him and kept walking. He threw his towel into the large plastic bin at the end of the pool and felt someone pull at his arm. Without thinking it through he spun around and grabbed the man by the neck.

"Don't you ever touch me! You got that? Don't ever touch me."

The man said nothing as Scott released his grip. He looked around to see several people watching the exchange. Remorse immediately settled in. *What the hell am I doing? I've never done anything like that in my life.*

Scott shook his head and put the bottle into the man's hands. "I'm sorry. I'm sorry. Here, for your trouble." Scott handed the man a twenty dollar tip and kept walking.

"Sir, here take this."

Scott turned and saw the man holding out the bottle with a stretched hand. A plastic cup was hanging upside down on the mouth of the bottle. "I just thought you might want a cup."

Scott bowed his head in embarrassment. *What the hell is my problem?* "Thanks amigo. Again, I'm sorry."

"No problem. You look like you need it."

"I do."

Scott returned to his room with a deep sense of guilt and alarm at what he had just done. His pulse had not settled and the tingling remained. He unscrewed the cap of the bottle and threw it across the room as he chugged as much as he could in one gulp. After almost vomiting he sat on the floor with his back against the wall and felt his head begin to swell. Tears were beading up in his eyes as he struggled to hold them back. He couldn't remember the last time he cried and tried not to think about it. *What is this? Why is this happening? Block it out. Block it out. Block it out. You can beat this.*

He finally surrendered. He could block it out no longer. He lay on his side as the tears burst from his face, a puddle forming within minutes on the tile floor below his head. He sobbed and rocked back and forth for over an hour, not fully knowing why he was crying. All of the emotions that he suppressed over the years came flowing back. The loss of his parents, the failed relationships and watching Diablo kill Frances. All of these incidents were out of his control, but he couldn't help feeling responsible.

He continued to drink from the bottle and couldn't remember if he finished it before passing out or if he had woken up and needed more. It didn't matter. The morning still brought with it a headache and subsequent embarrassment of monumental proportions.

Scott struggled to get to his feet and reached the bathroom seconds before vomiting. He kneeled on the tile floor with his face pressed against the cool porcelain of the toilet. He stared at his reflection in the mirror on the back of the bathroom door. *How did this happen to me? Six months ago I was a Special Forces soldier on top of the world. Now look at me.*

It took the better part of the morning to get himself together, bathe and pack. It was time to change locations again. Scott felt he had to keep moving, running, searching. His emotions were running wild and he felt his control over them slipping. The wall was weakening. He had to rebuild it, but questioned his ability to do so. He checked out and began driving again. His greatest fear was that no matter where he went, he would not be able to escape the painful memories of the past and the uncertainties of the future. A life without purpose is not a life.

Chapter 14

Cabrera, Dominican Republic

Scott continued to drive east. He felt he needed to get out of the resort areas for more seclusion. He needed to find a place to gather his thoughts, and strengthen his emotions. After stopping several times to vomit, he decided to stop for some much needed food. After entering the town of Cabrera, he parked in the town square.

Scott looked around and liked the fact that the town was configured around the square. It was efficient and orderly, yet intimate and inviting. Scott's headache was almost gone, but his stomach cried for food. He couldn't wait for much longer and decided on something quick.

The hot dog and hamburger trailer on the north side of the square looked perfect. Scott had to knock on the side of the trailer to wake the man.

"Sorry amigo, but I need something to eat."

"No, no problem. You come to the right place. What can I get you?"

"Which is your specialty, the hot dogs or hamburgers?"

"Both."

I should have guessed. "Ok. Give me one of each and go easy on the grease."

Scott sat in one of the green plastic chairs next to the trailer and exhaled. His body was hurting and his mind was spinning.

"You want a drink?"

Scott thought for a minute. "Yeah, give me a beer."

The man threw Scott's hamburger and hot dog on the grill and reached into his cooler to retrieve a cold beer. He delivered it with a napkin wrapped around the outside and another one placed over the top of the bottle.

"Gracias."

"Siempre."

Ten minutes later Scott was finished with his food. He needed to fill his stomach, having vomited everything out of his system. The man had pulled up a chair next to Scott, but said nothing.

"So, what goes on in this town?"

"Here? Nothing really. We get a few tourists, but not many, mostly day trippers. The beach is close, about one thousand meters that way," he pointed as he spoke. "There are a few places to stay, mostly guest houses. Are you passing through?"

Before Scott could answer he saw a young woman walk slowly out of the restaurant two houses down from the trailer. She walked gracefully as she surveyed the outside tables and gave directions to the waiters who moved the furniture around according to her wishes. Scott was stunned.

"What? I missed that. What was your question?"

The man looked at Scott's eyes then turned his head to follow his gaze towards the woman. He smiled. "I asked if you were staying or passing through."

Scott did not answer. He was completely captivated by the woman at the restaurant. This was rare, if not a first. Scott had traveled all over the world, seen the most beautiful women in existence and had never been so enamored.

"Who is that woman?"

"That's Esperanza de la Cruz. She owns the restaurant."

Scott looked to the entrance of the restaurant and read the sign, *Esperanza's*. He watched her as she continued to rearrange the dining area. She had long dark hair down to the middle of her back and a vivacious figure. He had to get a closer look.

"Listen, she's not married and hasn't had a boyfriend that I know of, ever. But unless you're the church going type, which I doubt you are, you don't have much of a chance."

He continued to talk as Scott got up from his chair and ignored him.

"Hey amigo! Don't go now! You need to clean up a bit, take a chicklet or something!" He shrugged his shoulders and muttered to himself. Then he spun his chair around so he could watch the action.

Scott ran his fingers through his hair and scratched his beard. He opened the gate to the walkway and climbed up the stairs to the restaurant. Scott stood at the top of the stairs with a blank expression on his face. She was wearing spotless white pants, a blue silk blouse and open toe shoes that showcased her meticulously painted toes. *If angels existed, which they don't, they would look like her.*

Scott stood speechless until she noticed him. He was wearing torn shorts, flip flops and a Special Forces t-shirt. His hair was unkempt and his beard was scraggly. She looked him up and down and he immediately felt self conscious. *Maybe the hot dog guy was right. But it's too late now.*

"Can I help you?"

"Excuse me?"

"Can I help you?"

"Yes. I'd like a table please."

"We don't open on Monday's until dinner at five o'clock."

"I'll wait."

"It's twelve thirty and I don't think that's such a good idea. We have some rearranging to do."

"Can I help?"

"Oh, are you looking for a job?"

Scott's face turned red as he looked down at his appearance. "Actually no, but I sure could use a drink." He laughed as he said it, she didn't.

"This isn't a bar, it's a restaurant. If you'd like to eat you can come back when we're open. But for right now, you'll have to excuse me." She then smiled, turned and walked into the restaurant without looking back.

Scott stood speechless and motionless. He could not recall ever feeling so small. Two of the waiters who continued to move chairs wore smiles from ear to ear as they pretended not to notice. *Laugh it up boys, laugh it up.*

The hot dog man laughed out loud as Scott returned to his seat. "I tried to tell you man, you wouldn't listen."

"Give me another beer."

"My name is Jose," he said.

"Scott."

They shook hands before Jose entered the trailer and spoke as he grabbed another beer for Scott. "She's tough. She's had that restaurant for three or four years now and I've never seen her with a man. They all try, but nobody ever gets a second chance. Bro, if you're going to be here for a while I can introduce you to some sure things."

"Why? You don't think I can do that myself?"

"Well so far you aren't doing so well, but what do I know?"

"Jose, I need a place to stay for a few days. Do you know of any rooms?"

"Of course, my uncle owns that house over there, across the square from us. He's got an apartment on the second floor. It has a balcony too. Just tell him I sent you so I get my commission. Ok?"

"Sure. No problem." Scott guzzled his second beer, stood up and started walking towards his car. He probably wouldn't have had that second beer if he knew that Esperanza was watching him from inside the restaurant.

The apartment was fully furnished and Jose had been right, there was a balcony. Scott turned to Jose's uncle.

"I'll take it."

"How long will you be staying?"

"I'm not sure, probably just a few days." Scott flipped through his wad of money and peeled off some notes. "Here's three days rent. If I stay longer we can work something out right?"

"No problem. Enjoy." He handed Scott the key and left.

Scott unpacked his things and knew immediately it was time for laundry. He placed his things in the basket and put it outside the door for the maid to clean. His clothes would be cleaned and pressed before dinner.

Scott peeled off his clothes and walked into the bathroom for a shower. He emerged ten minutes later feeling a bit better, but a little on edge. He tried to forget his experiences from the day before. *Why did I grab that poor guy by the throat? And why did I explode back in my room?* Then he remembered the kiss that triggered his emotions and blocked it out. He couldn't let that happen again.

He decided to walk through downtown to check things out. There wasn't much to see, a few shops here and there, a grocery store, a bank and of course a church. Scott entered the grocery store and soon exited with a case of beer over his shoulder and a bottle of rum swinging in his left hand.

He was running low on cash so he crossed the street to visit the bank. The cash machine was guarded by an old man with a shotgun who smiled as Scott entered the ATM. As he waited for his money, he looked at his reflection in the screen. *I look like hell. This beard may have to go.* Scott took his money, folded it and placed it in his front pocket. He exited the bank and gave ten pesos to the security guard. *There's nothing wrong with a little good will.*

People were walking back and forth in the streets. Everyone he passed smiled and greeted him. *Nice town,* he thought to himself. As he crossed the square to return to his apartment, he noticed Esperanza standing in front of her restaurant watching him walk. She turned away before he could wave. Scott wondered what he must look like. *Good job Scotty, another great impression. I might as well write that one off.*

Scott entered his room and stuffed the entire case of beer into the refrigerator. Then he grabbed the bottle of Rum, turned on the radio and sat on the balcony. His emotions were creeping in again, so he swigged from his bottle and washed them away.

He woke up a few hours later in a soaking wet bed. He had initially fallen asleep on the balcony and then moved inside to the bed. His initial thought was that he had drunk so much that he lost control of his bodily functions, but after shaking out the cobwebs and getting a glass of cold water he realized the majority of the wetness was around his head and back. The air conditioning had been shut off, probably by the maid.

He poured himself a cup of water and walked out onto the balcony. Off to the side he noticed a spiral staircase leading to the roof. He jumped over the railing onto the stairs and climbed them to the top.

Although the roof was only slightly more than two stories high, it gave him an excellent view of the town square. He could see Jose sleeping next to his hot dog trailer, the lights in front of the bank, the supermarket and the flicker of candles from Esperanza's. Scott laughed to himself. *Man, I really turned her off. She looked downright disgusted with me.*

The back of the building offered a less beautiful view of several small side streets, but you could see the glimmer of the Atlantic Ocean beyond them. Tomorrow he planned on hitting the beach and getting some sun. *Maybe I'll stay for a week or so.*

Chapter 15

Terrorist Tracking Center (TTC) Richmond, Virginia

Smitty yawned as he reached for his fourth cup of coffee in the last hour. He had a headache, but that comes with the territory. Numbers and patterns had been burned into his mind from staring at computer screens over the past eight years. Rarely did he see the sunlight. Sometimes he slept on the couch in the TTC, put there for him especially by the director, Steven Barnes.

Tracking terrorists and the like was tedious at times. The programmer has little to do after the profile has been constructed. The software originated in the late nineties, but was automatically updated almost daily with new features. For Smitty it was like having a living and breathing tutorial with which to keep up. That was the exciting part, watching the new abilities evolve.

Targets were tracked through obvious channels like bank account activity, emails, and phone records, but this system went many steps further. It tracked the activities of the target's contacts and acquaintances and in the process could give the TTC a big picture of the circles in which the target communicated. It would then construct profiles and automatically add them to an ancillary watch list.

Any contacts with the ancillary contacts could then be probed and matches would be looked for. In the process, an inescapable trail of information could give the TTC a good indication of the primary target's location and activities; all done completely legally thanks to small, unknown parts of the Patriot Act. The system could also tap into surveillance cameras in banks and other places and retrieve snapshots. One such snapshot was now the cover page of The Xpatriot's file.

"You're not sleeping are you?" Barnes was now standing behind Smitty, who hated it when he would sneak up and watch him work over his shoulder.

"Not yet, but I was thinking about it."

"Not until I get my report."

Smitty grabbed the file next to him and handed it over his head without looking.

"That's more like it. What's the short version?"

"He's left Santo Domingo, rented a car and checked out of his hotel, the credit card records are attached. He's on the north coast now, as evidenced by the cash withdrawal in a small town called Cabrera. He's probably going to stay there."

"What makes you say that?"

"Because I looked into the town, there are no major resorts, mostly small bed and breakfasts that don't take plastic. Thus the cash withdrawal, but it's just a guess."

"Let's not guess Ok? This is high profile."

"Ok. Then look at the picture I lifted from the ATM. See the case of beer resting next to him? I doubt that's for the drive."

"Yeah well, anything else?"

"Not really. He's only checked his email once in the past week, mostly newsletters. No suspicious contacts, actually no contacts at all. He must be a lonely guy. No phone calls from the island that I'm aware of, but he could have used a different phone than his room and called a number not on the watch list."

"Nice picture. Didn't you get anything from that?"

"No. Looks like a miserable guy to me."

"Yeah well, my guess is he converted to Islam. See the beard? That's a dead giveaway. I know how these fugitives think."

Smitty rolled his eyes. "Hey there, Tommy Lee Jones, did you every think he's just being lazy?"

"I'm the analyst. You just get me the information. I don't have three congressional letters of commendation for nothing. This guy is dirty. I can feel it in my gut."

Smitty heard Barnes walk away behind him. *Yeah right. Look at the bloodshot eyes. How many Muslim extremists drink? What a jackass, Barnes. But who am I to ask questions? This guy must have done something wrong to get this type of attention.*

Chapter 16

Capital Building Washington D.C.

Senator Burke flipped through the file and shook his head. *What the hell are you doing? You look like Che Guevara for God's sake. America's finest huh? You look pathetic to me.*

Burke picked up his secure line and muttered to the operator on the other side. "Get me Viper."

"Right away, Sir." Thirty seconds passed and she spoke again. "Sir, I have Viper for you. At the tone your call is secure." Her voice was followed by a short beep.

"Viper here."

"You sure about this guy Green? He's clean?"

"One hundred percent clean. It's pure coincidence that he's on the island. Is he still on the North Coast?"

"Yes, he is right now."

"Sir, I'd stake my career on it. He's clean and has no idea."

"Ok. But I swear if he heads south prior to the mission, I will give the order myself. He interfered once in my business. I won't tolerate it again."

"I understand that. And I'm not worried. Remember, I know this guy."

"I know, you keep reminding me. Ok Viper."

The Senator hung up and the line went dead. Burke closed the file and thought to himself. *You got in my way once kid, don't do it again.*

Chapter 17

▼

Cabrera, Dominican Republic

Scott rolled out of bed and stumbled to the bathroom. He turned on the faucet and splashed his face with cold water. His eyes were red and his beard was stringy. Days had turned into weeks. He had lost track of time altogether in his routine; get up, hydrate and run along the beach. He ate when he remembered. But he never forgot to drink. He cried often, but never knew why. He was out of control. The only thing that kept him going was watching Esperanza across the square from his balcony. She noticed him often, but never acknowledged him. He felt beneath her.

If she would just get to know me, we might actually hit it off. Then he would break down and wonder why anyone would want him. *Look at what I have been reduced to. Who would want this?*

When faced with a life of torture with no hope of escape, most will choose death. Scott had never thought of death, he was always too strong. Now, for the first time in his life, he wanted out. The pain had become unbearable. He had no plan, no hopes and no support. Pieces of him died with his parents and the rest with Frances. He felt like a hollow shell, no substance and no consistency.

Scott stumbled to the kitchen, almost falling twice, grabbed his bottle and a knife. He walked outside and hopped the balcony railing so he could climb up to the roof. *There's no need to make a mess in the apartment.*

Esperanza de la Cruz looked at her watch, it was almost 1AM and the staff had gone home. She rubbed her eyes, closed her accounting books and decided to call it a night. Business was good, but slow. Most would say it wasn't worth the amount of work that she had to put in, but it was all hers. She had built the restaurant on her own and was proud of her accomplishment. Nevertheless, the days were long and she needed rest.

With her bag slung over her left shoulder, she closed the front door of the restaurant behind her and fumbled for her keys so she could lock the door. The streets were empty. They usually were when she closed.

She locked the doors and started walking down the street towards her apartment. She lived alone and liked it that way. Never married and with few relationships under her belt, she had yet to find the man of her dreams and refused to settle. But it wasn't for lack of offers. She was flattered and propositioned almost daily. But usually by tourists and they are rarely a good lot to choose from.

Esperanza turned left onto her street and continued to walk at a leisurely pace until she heard the distinct sound of glass shattering. She stopped and turned, but saw nothing. *That's strange. Perhaps it was a cat playing in the garbage or a drunk rolling over on his bottle. Keep walking.*

She continued walking until she heard voices. She decided against looking back and quickened her pace towards the door to her apartment. With her right hand she reached into her bag for the keys and grabbed the key closest to the Dominican Flag keychain. That was how she remembered the apartment key in the dark. She identified it and pulled it out so she would be ready to open the door as soon as she arrived.

The voices got louder and she heard footsteps getting closer behind her. Instinct told her to run. And she did.

She ran the last half block to the front door of her apartment and scrambled to insert the key into the lock. She thought she almost had it when a set of hands grabbed her by the shoulders and spun her around abruptly.

"What's the rush baby?"

There were two of them. She had seen them earlier, walking back and forth in front of her restaurant. They were not from Cabrera.

"Get your hands off of me!"

"Shut up! I'll let you go when I'm ready." One of them held a broken bottle against her throat while the other looked at her with crazy eyes.

"What do you want from me?"

"Oh, we'll get to that. Don't rush it baby, we've got all night."

"There's money in the bag, and the keys to the restaurant. Take it! Take it and leave me alone!" They could hear the desperation in her voice.

"We will. But that's not all we plan on taking. You think you're better than us don't you?"

"No! No!"

"Yes you do. Admit to it. We're not good enough to taste you are we? Well, how about we just take what we want, huh? Then you can go pray about it on Sunday."

"No! Please don't. Just take the money, you can have everything. Just leave me alone." She began to sob and the first man put a hand over her mouth to muffle the sound.

"There, there little baby. Don't worry, I promise you'll enjoy this. I know I will."

They dragged her around the corner of her apartment building and into the alley. She tried to struggle, but stopped when the second man unleashed a closed fist punch into her kidneys, followed by a humiliating slap across the face.

"Please don't!" She begged one last time with blood trickling from her mouth.

"Why not? You know you want it and I don't see any witnesses. But let me guess, God is watching right? Is God watching?"

"He's always watching." Esperanza's voice was barely audible.

"What's that?"

"He's always watching." The tears streamed down her face.

"Well, I have to tell you, I don't see him anywhere." Both men started laughing quietly but loud enough for her to hear. The second man inched closer and gently licked the side of her tear soaked face. "Where is he baby? Where's God now?"

All three of them were surprised to hear a fourth voice. "I'm here."

The second man turned around quickly as Scott Green swung the half empty rum bottle, crashing it down onto the bridge of his nose. The man's knees buckled and his unconscious body dropped to the ground with a thud, the glass shattering. The other man threw a punch that caught Scott on the side of the head. Scott hesitated for a second, regained his balance and waited for another with his fists raised.

Landing one clean punch gave the assailant a false sense of security. "Hey gringo, hey gringo! Are you here to save the day, huh? Bring it!" The man swung wildly at Scott, who ducked and came up with an uppercut, breaking the man's jaw and causing him to bite his tongue. Blood sprayed everywhere as he fell to the ground. Scott maintained his stance and looked to make sure the other man was still down.

He watched as the assailant reached into his pocket and removed a blade before he stood up. "You're gonna die, Gringo!"

Scott responded by reaching behind into his back pocket and pulling out the knife from his kitchen.

The man hesitated for a second then lunged at Scott with the knife. Scott shuffled to the side, grabbed his knife bearing hand by the wrist and clothes lined him with the other arm. The assailant's feet came out from under him as if the rug had been pulled out. He landed on the concrete, the back of his neck breaking his fall.

Scott kicked the man's knife to the side and grabbed him by the hair, his other hand holding the knife against his throat. "Where's God now, brother? Where is he? Huh? You don't know?"

Esperanza was huddled in the alley against the wall. She stood up and slowly approached Scott. "Don't do it."

Scott continued talking to the man. "Tell me, tough guy. Huh? Where's God now? You're looking at him aren't you?"

The man could barely speak. "Yes. Yes. You are God."

"Wrong. There is no God." Scott held the knife up above his head and prepared to plunge it into the assailant's neck. Esperanza grabbed Scott's arm and screamed. "No! No! No! No killing! Don't be an animal!"

She pushed Scott to the side and stood between him and the assailant.

"Animal? This guy would have killed you, after raping you. And I'm the animal?"

"No killing! No killing! Stop! Just stop!" She dropped to her knees, bowed her head and cried uncontrollably.

Scott looked down at both men. "Well boys, you heard the lady. No killing." *Imagine that.* "Hey lady, I didn't make this. I didn't make this. I just fixed it. A little gratitude wouldn't kill you." Scott was huffing and puffing as he spoke. He looked back and forth between Esperanza and the man. He dropped the knife, made a fist and punched him as hard as he could directly in the temple. The man grunted as he lost consciousness.

Scott threw his knife into a garbage can and started walking away, wiping his hands on his pants. He muttered as he walked. He could hear the siren from the police car approaching, but he didn't care. He walked slowly back towards the apartment. *No killing. No killing. I need a drink.*

Chapter 18

Cabrera, Dominican Republic

Another morning brought another monumental headache. But this one wasn't supposed to come. *What the hell was that all about? Was it real? Was it a dream?* Scott lay in bed asking himself the same questions over and over when all he had to do was look at his blood soaked clothes next to the bed.

Another stumbling walk to the bathroom and another cold splash of water to the face woke him up. *Amazing, I need answers. How could she call me an animal after saving her life? I would have done the world a favor by taking both of them out.*

Scott showered and got dressed. For the first time in months he had a mission. He needed to talk to Esperanza. Was she ok? Did she know the assailants? Why did she call him the animal? She had to know that he was sorry if he went too far. *Too far? Come on! I saved her life. I want answers.*

The sunshine blinded Scott as he opened the front door to his apartment house. After instinctively pulling his sunglasses down from his forehead, he started walking across the square. The few people outside looked at him. Two men gave him the thumbs up. *Wow, it's a small world, but that's more like it. A little appreciation isn't too much to ask.*

It was 11:00AM as Scott climbed the stairs to Esperanza's and walked down the brick path towards the door. Before he could knock, the door opened. She stood in the threshold looking at him.

"Hi," he said.

"Hello."

"Are you ok?"

"Yeah, I'm fine."

"Good because I was…"

"Listen, thanks ok? I'm sure that's why you're here, so thank you."

Scott paused and pushed his sunglasses back on top of his head. "It helps, but that's not why I came. I came to see if you were ok. Does that hurt?" Scott pointed to the bruise on the side of her cheek.

She instinctively turned her head to the side to hide it and nodded. "Yeah, I'm fine. Look, thanks for the help. You probably saved my life, but I have to go."

"Fine, I just thought I would formally introduce myself. My name is…"

"Scott Green, yes I know, it's a small town. And you came for your thank you. Now you have it."

Scott stood speechless. *Wow, she hates me more than before I saved her.*

"Hey, would you like to get a drink or something to eat sometime?"

"I don't think that's a good idea. You and I are different people."

"How do you know?"

"I know your type."

Scott started to speak and then decided against it. He had never felt so insulted. He spoke slowly and deliberately. "You don't know me. You know nothing about my type. I just came to see if you were ok. Good luck." He pulled his sunglasses back over his bloodshot eyes, turned and walked away. She spoke before he reached the stairs.

"Ok, but not here. I've made it a policy not to socialize in my restaurant. Meet me at CoCo's at 7 o'clock. It's on the other side of town near the water."

Scott continued to walk and made no reaction.

"Did you hear me? 7 o'clock at CoCo's," she said louder.

"I'll think about it," he said over his shoulder. A smile grew across his face as he walked back to his room. *Of course I'll be there.*

Esperanza was seated at CoCo's at 6:55 and ordered a glass of white wine. She looked at her watch and exhaled, she was nervous. *If this guy doesn't show up, I'll never talk to another gringo for the rest of my life. Why am I here anyway? He's repulsive.*

The waiter smiled and placed a menu in front of her. "Will anyone else be joining you this evening?"

"I don't know, possibly."

She waited for twenty minutes and started to become more anxious. *What am I doing? This guy isn't coming.* As she held up her arm to signal the waiter for the check, she felt a soft touch on her shoulder. "Is this seat available?"

She turned around quickly, Scott was standing behind her. He was dressed in dark pants, shiny leather shoes and a white button down shirt. His hair had been cut and he was closely shaved. There was a faint smell of cologne and he smiled widely.

"Yes it is," she said.

Scott walked around the table and took his seat. He unfolded his napkin and placed it on his lap. Sitting up straight, he smiled.

"I'm sorry I'm late."

"Did you stumble upon a burning church full of orphans on the way?"

Scott laughed. "Wow. Was that humor? I like it."

"Yes it was and I'd like to apologize for this morning. I was rude and I had no right to treat you like that, especially after what you did for me."

"Don't mention it. You actually saved me."

"What does that mean?"

Scott recognized that he was thinking out loud. "Nothing, don't even think about it. I'm sure you would have done the same for me. So what's good here?"

"I haven't been here in a while, but I hear the ribs are good."

"I'll take your word for it," Scott said, as the waiter arrived and asked for his drink order.

"I'll have a glass of water please."

Esperanza tried to hide her surprise, but couldn't resist. "No drink for you?"

"Not tonight. I had a nice run today and I feel pretty good. But don't condemn me if I have a Baileys after dinner."

They made mostly small talk after ordering their dinner. Scott had the ribs and Esperanza the catch of the day. The service was courteous, but predictably slow. Scott asked about her family and where she grew up.

"I grew up right here in Cabrera. It's a small town, but I like it."

"Do your parents live here?"

"They did. My father left my mom when I was a baby. I've never spoken with him, but heard he died ten years ago. My mother was killed in a car accident eight years ago on my twenty second birthday."

Scott felt his pulse quicken. "I'm sorry. I wouldn't have asked."

"No it's ok. We were very close and I loved her very much, but I'm ok now. It was tough, but things happen for a reason and always have a way of working out."

"I guess they do."

"My mother was from Havana, Cuba. I have some relatives there, but other than them I've pretty much been on my own since I lost her."

"Do you have any kids?"

She stopped eating and looked at him directly in the eyes. "No, I've never been married."

"That doesn't exactly matter these days does it?" Scott said casually, as he continued to eat.

"It does to me."

That was a smooth move Scott. "That's not what I meant, I was just saying…"

"I know. I know. Don't worry about it. No, I have no children and have never been married. What about you?"

"No to both. My lifestyle thus far hasn't exactly been conducive to relationships." Scott gave a quick summary of his career, leaving out most of the details and being as vague as possible.

"So what brings you here to the DR?"

"I'm not really sure. I guess it's kind of a calling. I got out of the military and wanted to take some time to think before I made my next move. So far I've done more thinking than planning, but that's changing."

"It is?"

"Yes, as we speak." He cringed, this was his first attempt at flirting and he was prepared for the worst. She laughed. *Thank God. Wait, I don't believe in God. I guess I was lucky. Now back off and don't flirt again, don't look desperate or aggressive.*

They both ordered dessert. After finishing they sat back and breathed easy. He asked how she got started in the restaurant business. She related her story of starting out after high school as a hair dresser and saving her money in the hopes of someday opening her very own business. When she was ready the space was available. Scott took one more bite and then dropped his fork.

"That was great," he said.

"Yes it was. It's not the best in town, but its close," she said with a smile.

Scott smiled back, but said nothing as he sat and looked at her. *You are the most beautiful woman I have ever seen. There isn't a detail about you that I would change. You're an angel.*

"What are you thinking?"

"Nothing, I'm just relaxing."

"Well it's getting late for me and I have to be at work early tomorrow."

Scott held his hand up and politely motioned towards the waiter for the bill. As it arrived, Scott reached for his wallet and she reached for her purse. "No Scott. This one is mine. It's the least I can do."

Scott grabbed the check from across the table and said "Sorry, my mother would never forgive me." He glanced at the check, peeled off some bills and placed them in the black leather folder.

"She's not watching. Or is she?"

"Is who watching?"

"Is your mother watching?"

"I'm not sure, but I'd like to think so."

Esperanza could tell by his tone that his mother was dead and left it at that. "Thank you very much, it's unnecessary, but thank you."

"No problem. Let me walk you home."

She hesitated for a second then nodded her head. "Ok."

They strolled along the sidewalk talking about small things, both of them careful not to arouse unknown wounds from the past. There was a connection. People who have experienced tremendous loss can sense each other. They kept it light, but both felt the need to get the details from the night before out of the way.

The two men who assaulted Esperanza de la Cruz were brothers from a small town an hour away from Cabrera. The police had been looking for them for a month. They were wanted for rape and murder. Esperanza had kicked them out of her restaurant previously for being obnoxious and disrespectful to her employees. Scott just happened to be on the roof of his apartment when he saw them follow her home. When the police arrived, they were happy to have the men in custody, no questions asked. If it had happened in the U.S., the men could have sued Scott in civil court and would have had a chance at winning. Not in the DR.

"Here we are," she said nervously, as they arrived at the door to her apartment.

Scott looked around. "Yes we are. Thank you for your time, I enjoyed talking with you. It's been a long time since I've had a meaningful conversation and I appreciate it."

Scott held out his hand. She accepted it, stepped forward and kissed him gently on his cheek. He felt electrified. *You have no idea how bad I needed that.*

"Well then, I'll see you around."

"Yes you will," she said with a warm smile.

Scott turned and started walking home. After a few seconds he turned and spoke to her again. "Esperanza, do you know any good places in Cabrera for breakfast?"

She smiled and looked up, pretending to think. "Yeah, I'll be at work early. If you stop by I'll make you some eggs and coffee. If you're after something fancier you'll have to go elsewhere."

"Hmmm, that's a tough one. But I would like that very much."

She shut the door and he heard the door lock tightly. *Maybe there is a God.*

Chapter 19

Cabrera, Dominican Republic

Scott arrived at the restaurant at eight 'clock. The strong smell of Dominican coffee brewing in the kitchen was intoxicating. He sat on a stool next to the large stainless steel counters and talked with Esperanza as she cooked. She was wearing a dark blue halter top with matching skirt.

Her hair cascaded over her exposed shoulders, bouncing lightly whenever she turned her head from side to side, even more when she laughed. She wore flat sandals. He legs were toned, shiny and smooth, with not so much as a nick on them. It was starting to get hot in the kitchen when she reached up and effortlessly tied her hair into a pony tail. She was wearing no make up, but glowed in the morning sunlight. *Everything about her is perfect.*

"So you never told me anything about your family, Scott."

He paused for a second and responded. "Well, the story is not so different than yours."

He shared with her the details of the night his parents died, living with the Denuccis and becoming LTC McCallister's protégé. She continued to cook, but gave Scott her undivided attention.

"And that's about it. I've pretty much been on my own since."

You could see the empathy and sincerity in her eyes as she hung on every word. *Those eyes, I could get lost in them.* In her eyes he could see everything that was good in the world. Scott could see through them and into her heart, she was pure love.

"I have one question about the other night, after I'll let it go forever."

"Ok. What is it?"

"Why the sympathy? Why the mercy? After what they did and wanted to do, most people would want them dead. Wouldn't the world be a better place without them?"

She paused and looked at him directly in the eyes. "Is that our decision to make? Who lives and who dies?"

"Sometimes, yes."

"Not for me, God is the one with the authority to make those decisions."

"God? Are you serious?"

"Yes I am." She stopped cooking, and turned to face Scott.

"Where was God when our parents were killed? Where was God when those two pigs attacked you? For all the talk of this God, I've never actually seen him show up for anything."

"He's here, he's always here. Look, revenge is empty. All it does is contribute to the cycle. Believe me because I know."

"Tell me how?"

"The woman driving the car who killed my mother begged for my forgiveness. She was broken. I wouldn't even look at her. She tried almost daily for six months, I rejected her. She became a drunk and eventually hung herself. She had three daughters of her own and no husband. My failure to forgive orphaned three kids. I killed her and I'll have to live with that for the rest of my life. The cycle continued, but I could have stopped it."

Scott could see that he struck a nerve, but he understood. "I understand where you're coming from, I do. But there is a fine line between true justice and foolish revenge." He finished his breakfast in silence before he looked up again.

"So what are your plans today?" Scott asked.

"Work, work, work. Today should be busy and I'm thinking of rearranging the dining room again."

"Again?"

"Yes, again. Is that ok with you?" she asked sarcastically.

"Yes it is. Just let me leave before the heavy lifting starts," he said. She smiled and laughed.

"You are so beautiful when you laugh."

She tried to stop smiling, but couldn't. He was, after all, much more charming than she imagined possible. "I think the heavy lifting is about to begin," she said.

"That's my cue. I'm outta here." Scott hopped up from his stool and carried his plate and glass to the sink.

"Just leave that stuff right there."

"Ok. Thank you for breakfast and especially your company. I truly enjoy it."

"No problem."

"All right then. I guess I'll see you later." He leaned over and kissed her on the side of the cheek. *She smells like an angel too.*

She watched Scott from inside the restaurant as he walked across the town square. He waved and greeted everyone who he passed. They all seemed to know him. It was rare for a foreigner to be this accepted. Esperanza thought to herself. *Scott Green is something special.*

Scott spent the bulk of the morning doing errands. He withdrew some cash from the bank, bought a cell phone and went to the local internet café. This one was better than the café in Santo Domingo. It was close to the water and a nice breeze kept it cool. Scott sent Tony Denucci an email and decided to follow it up with a phone call.

"Hey big boy."

"Scott! How the hell are you man?"

"I've never been better. How's business?"

"I have no complaints. Where are you?"

Scott brought him up to speed on the past few weeks. "And as of right now, I have no plans. I like this town and might stay for a bit longer. Also, I have met the most beautiful woman in the world."

"Really? A woman? Are you sure this time?"

"Very funny, but not even your sophomoric humor can bring me down this time."

"Sounds like you're having a good time. Keep in touch."

"I will."

Chapter 20

▼

Terrorist Tracking Center (TTC) Richmond, Virginia

Smitty was surfing back and forth through comic book websites and learning about the newest capabilities of the TTC system when he decided to check on the Xpatriot file.

"Here we go."

Smitty backed out of the files that he was working with and opened the one entitled Xpatriot. *Ok, Ok...a call to Denucci...very good...new cell phone number...that provider has three major zones on the island...this call was serviced through the northern zone...he must still be on the North Coast...look to banking...withdrawal this morning at the same bank...retrieve photo...no beard...must have been hot as hell with that thing on your face...or maybe you met a chic...email records...ah hah...more contact with Denucci...from a new hotmail account...trace the IP...come on, come on...this is slow...there it is...ISP provider accounts...bingo!...downtown Cabrera...so, now I have your email, new cell phone and updated pic...damn I'm good.*

All Level One Red files were to be updated in real time. Major changes needed to be brought to the attention of the supervisor. Smitty made the proper changes with supporting documentation and picked up the phone to let Barnes know that the updated file was on his desk if he cared to come in on a Saturday. *Yeah right, Barnes on a Saturday. That'll be the day. He's probably on another one of his internet dates. I love reading his email records!*

Chapter 21

Cabrera, Dominican Republic

Scott changed into his running clothes and took off heading away from the town square. It was hot and the sweat felt good. He had spent fifteen minutes stretching and doing calisthenics before leaving the apartment and it was paying off. He was limber.

What a couple of days. I feel alive again. I think I'm in love. And she doesn't hate me. That's a good start. Scott channeled his hopes and dreams into his workout and quickened his pace. After one hour he was surprised and elated to see that he had almost doubled his usual running distance and shaved minutes off of his time.

He climbed to the roof of his apartment and exercised vigorously for the next twenty minutes without resting. Pushups, sit-ups, mountain climbers, crunches…Pushups, sit-ups, mountain climbers, crunches…Pushups, sit-ups, mountain climbers, crunches. *Damn, that's amazing. My shoulder didn't throb once. It has to be her. She's good for me. Don't screw this up Scott. Do not screw this up.*

Esperanza was randomly checking in on her customers, asking them about their meals and the quality of their service. She approached the back table. Someone was reading the newspaper and held it up in front of them so they could make better use of the sunlight. She could not see who it was.

"Good morning. I'm sorry to bother you. I just wanted to check and make sure everything was all right."

Scott was smiling widely holding a cigar in his teeth when he lowered the paper. "Yes, everything is top shelf. It's one of my favorite places."

She smiled. "There's no smoking here."

"Come on lady, we're outside," Scott replied with a chuckle.

She reached across the table and gentle took the cigar from his mouth. "You heard me, no exceptions. Smoking is bad for you and it stains your teeth. Nobody will want to kiss you."

"Well I haven't exactly been bombarded with offers lately."

"Stop smoking and maybe your luck will change. I'll take care of this for you, enjoy your breakfast." Her smile lit up the entire dining area as she turned and walked away.

Scott finished his meal, paid his bill and walked inside the restaurant. Esperanza was in the back of the inside dining area and waved him over. He pulled out a chair across from her and sat down.

"I thought maybe you had left town."

"You thought or hoped?"

"Neither, I just hadn't seen you."

"I'm still here. I like it here. Hey, you work too much."

"No I don't. I just do what needs to be done. Maybe you work too little."

"That's definitely true. But still, why don't you take the afternoon off and go to the beach with me? Come on, it'll be fun."

"I can't. I have a lot of work to do and this is usually a busy day. Hector needs me here."

Scott stood up and called out for Hector. Esperanza held her head in her hands and spoke. "What are you doing?"

Hector approached and stood in front of Scott. "Hector, do you mind if the boss takes some time off this afternoon? Can you hold down the fort for a few hours?"

"Of course."

"Thank you," Scott said, as he sat back down in his chair. "See? No problem. I'll be back at twelve o'clock to pick you up. We can walk down together."

Esperanza smiled and nodded her head. *Maybe I do need to relax a little.*

Scott tried not to stare as Esperanza removed her shirt and shorts so she could apply sunscreen. She was flawless. He was speechless and thought to himself. *Ok, there is definitely a God.*

Her reaction was quite different when Scott took off his t-shirt. "Ouch, that's got to hurt."

"Not as much as it used to. But it still gets a little sore."

"What happened?"

"Afghanistan happened, a guy named Diablo happened."

"You believe in the devil, but not God?"

"Diablo is a person, forget about it. Let's swim, I'll race you to the water."

Scott took off in a full sprint towards the water. There weren't many people on the beach, mostly locals. Music came from a small hut situated in the center of the tree line. He reached the water and dove in head first. It was nice and cool.

When he emerged he looked back at Esperanza who was walking slowly and confidently. "I guess you win. You Americans are so competitive, even against yourselves."

"Very funny," Scott said, as he approached Esperanza with a mischievous look on his face.

"What are you up to? Don't even think about it."

Scott ignored her wishes and stood up in the shallow water. She made one last plea. "No Scott, I'll go in on my own."

"Too late, you disparaged my heritage. Now you have to pay."

He scooped her up with both hands, draped her over his good shoulder, walked towards the deeper water and dumped her. She came to the surface with a scowl on her face.

"You'll pay for that one Scott. Trust me."

"What? No forgiveness? Turn the other cheek my dear."

"Don't joke about that." She maintained her scowl for another minute or so, but then it turned to a smile. "Thanks for getting me out of work."

"No problem. You need to stop and smell the roses every once in a while."

The rest of the afternoon was spent lying in the sun, talking and joking. Scott had never imagined that the same woman who looked at him with such contempt now actually seemed to be enjoying his company.

She could not believe how badly she had misjudged Scott during their first encounter. At five o'clock they collected their things and began slowly walking back to the town square.

"I wonder how Hector is doing."

"I'm sure he's doing fine."

As they approached the restaurant, Hector came walking out quickly. "Esperanza, two members of the staff have called in sick for tonight. I tried to get replacements, but nobody is available. We have several reservations and one anniversary dinner, but I don't think we'll be able to handle it."

Esperanza turned to Scott. "See what happens when I disappear for a few hours?"

"What can I do to help?" asked Scott.

"Nothing. Thank you, Hector, I'll be inside in a minute and we'll figure something out."

Scott looked over and waived at Jose who was sitting next to his hot dog trailer. Jose gave the thumbs up sign and smiled broadly. Scott looked back at Esperanza.

"Thanks for the day, but I have to go. It looks like it's going to be a long night for me."

"Yeah, me too."

"Why?"

"You're looking at your new bartender. I'll be back in an hour to prep and I won't take no for an answer."

"Scott, do you even know how to bartend?"

He looked at her and pretended to be offended. "Please, I can do this in my sleep. I'll see you in thirty minutes." She shook her head and went to work.

Exactly thirty minutes later Scott entered the restaurant and went directly to the bar. He didn't announce his arrival, but instead went straight to work locating everything he would need for the night. The bottles were in a different order than a standard American bar so he rearranged them. One of the busboys stood next to him asking questions. Scott took advantage of the opportunity and taught the boy why the bottles needed to be in a more logical sequence. The boy nodded in agreement and acted as an assistant.

Esperanza walked into the restaurant wearing a cocktail dress. Scott looked up from the bar and spoke. "What can I get you?"

She smiled, reached out and touched his hand. "Thank you so much, you're a lifesaver."

"No, actually you're the lifesaver."

The night went off without a hitch. Scott, although out of practice, was the most efficient bartender the staff had ever seen. During several periods of time when the wait staff was busy, Scott would leave the bar and take drink orders from the dining room. The staff was elated and Esperanza had time to float about and supervise.

By twelve O'clock the restaurant was empty and the staff was cleaning up. Esperanza was at the far table closing out the books.

"Scott, this was one of the best nights I've had this season. Thank you for the help. I have to pay you."

He spun around, "No way. I will not accept anything for this. I did it to help out. Besides, I've been stealing Cokes all night."

"Thank you so much. I appreciate you doing this."

"I did it for you." They held each other's gaze longer than usual until she blushed and went to check on the kitchen.

Each of the staff members made a point to stop and thank Scott personally on their way out. Scott waited for Esperanza to finish her work.

"The bar is all set for tomorrow. Let me walk you home."

"That sounds good, my feet are killing me."

They walked in relative silence as they turned the corner towards Esperanza's apartment. She reached into her bag for her keys as she spoke.

"Can I ask you a question?"

"Of course."

"What did you mean when you said I was a lifesaver? You sounded serious, it struck me as odd."

Scott hesitated and thought for a few seconds. "When I was up on the roof of my apartment and saw those two guys following you." He paused.

"Yes?"

"I wasn't exactly having constructive thoughts about my life. In fact, I wanted to end it. But then I saw you and couldn't bare the thought of someone hurting you."

She looked deep into his eyes, placed her hand on his cheek and kissed him firmly on the lips. Then she pulled back, looked him in the eyes and kissed him again. "Thank you."

"Esperanza, I have to warn you."

"Warn me? Why?"

"I'm falling in love with you. If you don't think it could ever work, please tell me now and I'll leave."

"Leave? No, Scott. I need my bartender." She smiled and blew him another kiss before entering her apartment and locking the door behind her. Scott smiled too. *I'm not falling, I've fallen.*

Chapter 22

Cabrera, Dominican Republic

The next few weeks were the happiest in Scott's entire life. He ate all of his meals at Esperanza's, with her, and filled in at the bar at her request. The staff welcomed him daily with open arms and never got used to him helping them with even the most menial of tasks. Physically, he was back in shape. He had found purpose again and had Esperanza to thank for everything.

Esperanza felt the same way. He had filled a void in her life that she never thought would be filled. But she maintained an internal struggle. Her Christian faith was unwavering, a noble trait in the eyes of God, but inconvenient in the modern world. She felt herself growing closer and closer to Scott but had never previously even considered a relationship with an atheist. They said "I love you" to each other daily and meant it, but otherwise controlled their passions.

She had spent many hours thinking about Scott and his comments about God. He sometimes refused to see the positives in life, too busy focusing on the negative. It was time for them to talk about it before they went any further.

Scott was reading one of the painfully boring books left in the apartment when he heard Esperanza call for him from the square. He stepped out onto the balcony and looked down at her.

"Are you awake? Can I talk to you?"

"Absolutely, come on up."

After greeting with a warm hug and kiss, they small talked for a few minutes and Esperanza asked if they could go up onto the roof. Scott grabbed two wine glasses and what was left of a bottle of Chardonnay. He helped her over the railing and they climbed onto the roof.

"What a beautiful night," he said.

"It is. I wish I had a roof like this."

"You can use mine anytime you'd like."

"Scott there's something I need to talk to you about, but I don't want to alienate you."

"Esperanza, you couldn't alienate me if you wanted to. You're stuck with me."

"Why don't you believe in God?"

Scott bowed his head and exhaled. "I've been waiting for this."

"I'm sorry. It's important to me."

"I know, I know. Listen, it's not exactly that I don't believe in God entirely. But if he exists, I question his actions and lack thereof. If he is all knowing and loving why does he let such awful things happen? Not just to me and you, but to the world. I mean look around, you have to look close to see the beauty."

"I don't think so. I look out the window and see beauty. Maybe you, and don't take this the wrong way, focus on the bad and overlook the big picture."

"In the big picture I have no family and have seen a lot of death and destruction. What good side is there to that?"

"Think about it."

"I'm thinking, but I still don't see it."

"God could have stopped all of that, it's true. But why should he? People deny his existence and fail to see the beauty of life. Some things have to happen so other things can happen. I don't claim to know it all, but I do believe that everything happens for a reason and he is always with us."

"Really? He's always here? Maybe I should have brought up three glasses." Scott could see by her expression that she was upset. "I'm sorry, I don't mean to make light of this. And believe it or not but being with you has made me think about this a lot lately. But I'm not there yet. Where was God when my parents were killed, and my friend was executed right in front of me? Where was God when I was shot? Where was he?"

She raised her voice. "Where was he? He was with you!"

Scott looked into her eyes. They were welling up with tears, but none had begun to roll down her beautiful face. "With me," Scott said quietly, as he shook his head in disbelief.

"Yes, haven't you ever wondered why you weren't in the car with your parents?"

"My mother made me help the janitors set up for graduation."

"Why didn't Diablo kill you? You got shot, but you lived!"

"Because he's a bad shot, I don't know why."

She knelt down in front of him, held his hand and looked into his eyes. "Why did you come onto this roof the night you saved me?"

"You know why."

"Tell me."

"I was going to kill myself."

"Why didn't you?"

"I don't know. It doesn't matter, I didn't."

"It does matter, tell me. What stopped you? Why didn't you do it?"

"Ok, that's enough for tonight."

"No it's not. Tell me, what did you do right before you were going to kill yourself?"

Several minutes passes as Scott contemplated answering the question. It would negate most of his argument. He finally answered. "I prayed."

"Why? Why would you pray to a nonexistent God?"

Scott's head was beginning to swell and tears formed in his eyes. He knew where she was going with the conversation, but didn't know if he was ready. "I asked him for a sign."

"What kind of sign?"

"Anything, something that would prove his existence to me."

"And what did he give you."

"I heard a break a bottle break and looked down to see two thugs following you."

"So what sign did he give you?"

"I don't know."

"Yes you do."

"He gave me you." Scott said as he looked deep into her eyes. She wrapped her arms around him and whispered into his ear.

"Do you know what Esperanza means in English?"

"Yes."

"It means hope. You asked and he gave you hope."

"I know. But it's so hard to believe after so long."

"It's never too late. Listen to this, Scott. About two months ago I was at work. I wanted to rearrange the patio furniture, yet again. But before going outside I prayed to God. And I asked for my knight in shining armor, like all women want from the time that we're little girls. Do you know what he gave me?"

"No."

"He gave me a gringo in shorts who needed a shave."

They both needed the levity and laughed out loud. "Things aren't always how they appear. But there is one thing I'm certain of, God is always with us. He brought us together at precisely the right second in order to save both of our lives. Everything that happened in our lives prior to that second was preparation. Everything happened for a reason. Sometimes people die so that others live and sometimes we can't see the big picture. That's when we have to put our faith in God and love."

"I know. I know. I love you." Scott held her tightly and whispered it several more times into her ear. She would never grow tired of hearing it.

Scott took an especially long run the next morning. He had a lot to think about. Esperanza had changed his life more than he could have ever imagined. He couldn't imagine life without her. She was beyond perfect, she was pure. It was time to profess his love in the form of a lifelong commitment.

He took the car to the next town over to browse through a few jewelry stores. There were several in Cabrera, but in such a small town she would have known of his intentions before he could leave the store. In the third store he found the ring that he felt was right for them.

Esperanza was not a flashy person and this one seemed perfect. It was a gold band with embedded diamonds all around. It was beautiful, would not get in the way of her work, and Scott could afford it. He paid for the ring, denied the owner's offer to wrap it and returned to the car.

It was hot. He started the car, blasted the air conditioning and closed his eyes. *Thank you God, thank you. You have made my life complete and I will never doubt you again.*

When Scott entered the restaurant it was late in the morning. Esperanza was sitting at the back table making the schedule. She wore her hair in a pony tail and was dressed casually. There was a quiet confidence in her as she looked up and greeted Scott.

"Hello handsome."

"Hi," Scott said, as he leaned over and kissed her before sitting down.

"I was expecting you for breakfast. Did you have a better offer?"

"Not at all, I just had some things to do."

"I see. Well, I ate a small breakfast, left shortly thereafter and I bought you something."

Scott stared at her expressionless. "You bought something for me?"

"Yes I did. And I know I'm taking a chance but here it goes." Esperanza reached into her bag and removed a long thin case. She pried it open and pushed it across the table to Scott.

Scott looked down at the case. Shining in the morning sunlight was a solid gold cross and necklace. He removed it from the case, held it up and looked at it without speaking.

Esperanza was anxious and curious. "Do you like it? I know you don't wear jewelry, but I wanted you to have this, as a reminder. I love you, Scott and God is always with you. If you ever doubt either, just look down." She sat and waited for a reaction.

Scott held the necklace with one hand. His other hand was in his pocket and held the ring for Esperanza. He thought to himself before he spoke. "I love it, and I love you too. It's perfect. Should I put it on now?" He released the ring from his fingers and rested his elbows on the table.

"Of course," she said, as she stood and leaned across the table. She opened the clasp and grasped the ends of the chain with both hands and held it in front of her for a second.

Scott looked at her. She seemed to glow in the sunlight with a peaceful smile across her lips. He looked into her charcoal eyes and saw the reflection of the cross sparkling in both of them. *I will never forget this moment.*

They were interrupted by Hector. "Esperanza, I can't fix it. We need a new motor. I can transfer all of the food to the other refrigerator, but we're expecting a delivery tomorrow and will need both. If not, the produce and meat will go bad."

"Great,' she said sarcastically.

"What happened?" Scott asked.

"The motor in one of the refrigerators burned out. The warranty is expired and the only place with parts is in the capital. Will they deliver it?"

"Yes, but they won't have the part until tomorrow morning and can't deliver until the next day," replied Hector.

"That won't do. We have some big parties this week and will need the refrigeration."

Scott put his hand on Esperanza's. "No problem, I'll take a ride down there this afternoon and spend the night. I'll pick up the motor first thing in the morning and will be back by noon. It's an easy in-and-out."

"No, I can't ask you to do that. Let me send one of the staff."

"And leave yourself shorthanded? Listen, it'll be a nice ride. I'll go down and be back for lunch tomorrow, no problem."

"Are you sure?"

"Of course I'm sure. I'm going to go pack an overnight bag. I'll take my time driving down. Really, I could use the change of scenery for a night."

"Ok. Thanks Scott, you're the best."

Chapter 23

Santo Domingo Dominican Republic

Scott packed a bag with a change of clothes and his toiletries. He was about to leave the apartment when he returned to grab his workout clothes. *A nice jog through Santo Domingo tonight will help me get to sleep early.*

The trip took him just over three hours. *That's pretty good, especially since I was taking my time.* The traffic got thicker as Scott weaved his way in and out of the narrow streets on the north side of the Capital. It took longer than he expected to reach his old hotel, but it was late afternoon and rush hour was coming.

The woman at the front desk smiled as Scott entered the lobby carrying only his backpack. "Hola! You're back. Did you like the north coast?"

"Yes, very much. I've decided to stay there."

"Good, good. That's normal. Gringos come for vacation and end up staying. You must be in love."

Scott ignored her probing. "Do you have a room available for the night?"

"Yes. Would you like the same one?"

Scott thought for a second. "No thanks. Actually, can you give me a different one?" Since meeting Esperanza his life had changed, he had no desire to look back. *Out with the old and in with the new.*

The air conditioning hummed loudly as Scott turned it on. He changed into his workout clothes and threw his backpack on the chair in the corner. *I'll have a nice early evening run, return to the cool room, then order a pizza and go to sleep. That's the plan.*

Scott was amazed at how far his physical rehabilitation had come since his first run in Santo Domingo. He covered the same distances at greater speeds and with less discomfort. *Amazing, I feel like a new man.*

He decided against heading back to the room for now and headed north on Avenida Maximo Gomez. Scott looked up the avenue and welcomed the challenge. The incline was slow and gradual, but long. He pumped his arms and legs and dug down deep. The rush was therapeutic. He was on top of the world.

At the top of the hill the road leveled off for the last quarter mile to the traffic light. The large four way intersection was home to one of Santo Domingo's only pedestrian overpasses. People walked back and forth fifty feet above the traffic.

Scott decided not to climb the stairs to the overpass to cross the busy intersection. Instead, he would stay in the ground level and turn right at the lights. He passed four of the white hat VIP traffic stoppers on his right hand side and waived to them, they waived back lazily. They were a friendly, but undisciplined looking group.

Scott continued for another block, waited for a break in the traffic and sprinted across to the north side of the street. After two more blocks he turned around and decided to start running back towards the hotel. He was drenched in sweat and was looking forward to the easy jog down the hill that he had previously conquered.

As Scott approached the intersection with Avenida Maximo Gomez he glanced to his left at the white hats. When he reached the bottom step of the overpass stairs he paused to run in place, but didn't know why. *Something isn't right here. What's going on?*

He continued running in place and turned again to face the intersection. The white hats were on the other side of the street talking to each other as they entered the intersection holding up their hands for the traffic to stop. *Something definitely isn't right.* And then he noticed.

These were not the same four undisciplined looking white hats that Scott passed only ten minutes earlier. They looked entirely different. *What's different with these guys? Where are the four clowns I saw before?* Scott continued to run in place but slowed his pace as he realized the differences. The four men entering the intersection were all armed. Two of them possessed side arms while the other two were toting shotguns. *This is weird. I've never seen an armed white hat. And why would they change the four on duty just minutes before stopping the traffic?*

Each of the four men took one of the four approaches to the intersection and raised their hands to stop the traffic. Scott watched from the bottom of the overpass. He could hear the sirens of the approaching caravan of VIPs. Several cars from each direction ignored the white hats and quickly darted across the intersection before they could be stopped.

Finally the intersection was clear, ready for the caravan to pass through. Then something inexplicable happened. As the caravan made its final approach to the intersection, all four white hats waved for traffic to continue simultaneously. Dominican drivers do not hesitate when given the right of way and quickly filled the intersection. The result was gridlock. The caravan was in the middle of pure chaos, unable to move.

The caravan consisted of three vehicles, two large SUVs in front and back of a large limousine with tinted windows. Horns could be heard throughout the intersection. The occupants of the lead SUV screamed into the vehicles' megaphone to clear the way.

The white hats moved slowly and deliberately. Two walked until they were in front of the lead SUV and began to act as if they were arguing and placing blame for the traffic jam. The other two quietly moved behind the rear SUV and waited.

The security detachment leader in the lead vehicle finally had enough and exited the vehicle. He approached the two white hats unleashing a fury of profanities and orders. His face was red. Veins bulged from his neck and forehead.

When he was within reach of the white hats, one of them turned towards him. A shotgun blast followed as the man was blown back several feet. He collapsed in a bloody heap. Before the other passengers in the lead SUV could react, both white hats opened fire. The driver and front passenger were killed in their seats. The security man in the back seat managed to exit the vehicle before being shot in the head.

The other two white hats approached the rear security vehicle from behind and emptied their weapons into the passengers. None could exit the vehicle to avoid the massacre. People were panicking and driving out of the intersection any way they could. Pedestrians on the overpass were running, none were looking. Basic survival instincts took over as people fled the scene.

Two plain clothes security men exited the limousine with pistols drawn, but were cut down before they could return fire. The white hats were in charge and had planned their ambush well. The two who had gunned down the rear security vehicle checked to make sure their targets were dead and ran down the street, fleeing the scene. The other two approached the limousine, one on each side.

The driver of the limousine could not move the vehicle, there were too many other cars maneuvering to exit the kill zone. He sat in his seat with his hands above his head, praying under his breath, begging for mercy. One white hat stood looking at him through the glass with a smile on his face, obviously enjoying the situation. He raised his pistol and fired into the driver's chest. He then turned to the other assassin who was on the other side of the limousine.

"Do it Jose! Do it quickly!"

Jose raised his shot gun and tapped the metal barrel against the glass of the limousine. The electric window opened as he chambered another shell. He pointed the barrel at the head of the man in the limousine and prepared to squeeze the trigger to accomplish his mission.

After sprinting thirty yards from the bottom of the steps to the limousine, Scott Green's elbow connected with the side of Jose's neck. He heard it snap as they both hit the ground. Scott hit his head on the pavement and was disoriented, but regained his senses within a few seconds.

The remaining white hat saw what happened. He held his pistol at the ready as he ran around the side of the limousine. The last thing he saw as he rounded the corner was Scott Green lying on his back with the shotgun pointed in his direction. A loud blast followed, then darkness. Scott was trying to catch his breath. *I had to shoot him. It was him or me, maybe more would have died. I had to do it. I had to do it. God forgive me.*

Scott turned his head and looked at the man on the ground next to him. He was unconscious. Scott opened the breech of the shotgun and saw that there was one shell left. As he closed the breech the rear door of the limousine opened.

A very well dressed and distinguished looking man exited the limousine and walked until he was standing over Scott.

"I demand to know who you are."

"I'm a tourist. Who the hell are you?"

The man was taken aback and then spoke proudly. As he was speaking, Scott shielded his eyes from the sun to get a better look at him. He recognized him from the newspapers as he heard the words. "I am the president of the Dominican Republic."

"Sir, you need to get back into the car and get down. This may not be over."

"I will not cower like a dog for these thugs. Who are you?"

Scott's eye was caught by something on the pedestrian overpass above. He looked over the president's shoulder and saw a man with a rifle pointed at the president's back. His scope reflected the sunlight. "Get down!" Scott shouted, as he raised the shotgun and squeezed the trigger. The man's rifle twirled and fell to the street below. The shooter's motionless body slumped over the rail.

Instinctively, Scott got to his feet and pushed the president back into the limousine. He walked to the front passenger door and opened it to check on the condition of the driver. The driver was bleeding profusely from the abdomen, but was conscious and indicated that he could drive the short distance to the Presidential Palace. Scott was surprised to find a short, fat, balding man curled up on the floor of the front seat. He reached down and grabbed the man by the shirt.

"Are you ok?"

The man was shaking and too scared to answer. Scott let go of his shirt and climbed into the back of the limousine. He banged on the glass divider and yelled.

"Vamos! Vamos!" He then turned to the president. "Sir, get on the floor."

"I will not…"

Scott cut him off. "Get on the floor before I start regretting helping you!"

The president looked insulted, but obeyed. He was obviously not accustomed to taking orders. Scott banged on the glass until someone in the front seat lowered the divider.

"How far is it to a secure location?'

"It's only five or six blocks. I have already called ahead and they are awaiting us," replied the bald man in the passenger seat. The driver managed to weave in and out of the remaining cars in his path. He pushed the accelerator to the floor as soon as he reached the open road. Scott was weary and thought out loud.

"There could be a contingency ambush, keep your eyes open."

"Who are you?" asked the balding man.

"I'm a tourist. Who are you?"

"I am the director of the president's security detail."

Scott rolled his eyes. "You're doing a real bang up job, buddy."

The gates to the Presidential Palace swung open as the limousine turned the corner. Dozens of soldiers and other security forces engulfed the vehicle as it stopped in front of the main entrance. The president was pulled from the back seat and taken directly to his emergency medical staff inside. Scott opened the door closest to him and was immediately slammed against the side of the car by several men. They were all screaming and yelling at the same time. It was impossible to understand them.

Scott was handcuffed behind his back and dragged into the palace. He tried to speak several times, but was either slapped or otherwise discouraged. The crowd of men didn't seem to know what to do with him and Scott could not figure out who was in charge. They were all barking orders at the same time.

Forty five minutes passed and there was still no consensus on what to do with Scott. They were all standing in a long, narrow hallway. Silence came over the crowd slowly and Scott could see the crowd parting as the president approached. He looked at Scott and then whispered something into the balding man's ear.

The man responded by telling everyone to return to their posts, the palace and military were to be placed on high alert. He also dismissed the two men who were holding Scott by his arms. He grabbed Scott by the left arm and spoke to him.

"Follow me. Do not say anything, just follow me."

"Do I have a choice?"

"No."

They walked down the long hallway, turned several times and entered what appeared to be a small office. The president was waiting inside. He was calmer now and smoked a cigarette as he motioned to remove Scott's handcuffs.

"So you are a tourist?"

"Yes, I am."

"And what is your name?"

"Scott Green."

"You are not typical of the tourists we are accustomed to in my country."

"I am not accustomed to this type of country as a tourist, Sir."

The president smiled and motioned for Scott to sit and the balding man to leave the room. He was visibly hurt by the request, but obliged.

"Are you hurt?"

"No sir. Just some cuts and bruises, but I'll be fine. Are you hurt?"

"My ego is bruised. The opposition party is made up of cowardly dogs. I have never taken their threats seriously. Maybe I should have."

The phone in the office rang and the president answered. He mostly listened. When he hung up the phone he looked at Scott, but did not speak for several minutes. He was deeply saddened and held his face in his hands before he spoke. He chose his words very carefully.

"I have lost ten of my closest security men and cabinet members. This is a sad day for the Dominican Republic and for me personally. I was the target and they died protecting me. Isn't that right Mr. Green? They died protecting me didn't they?"

Scott considered the president's words before he replied. "Yes sir, they died protecting you."

"And it is due to their heroism that I have survived this barbaric attack."

Scott understood exactly where he was going with this. He spoke very slowly. "Yes. They saved your life. The country and their families can be proud of them."

The president sat back and lit another cigarette. "Being the president of this country is not easy. There are many forces that work against you. Some of them are controllable, some are not. A man must have many qualities for this job, but principal among them is strength. You see, weakness begets weakness. Enemies can smell weakness and exploit it. Weakness is the kiss of death for a developing democracy. And having my security forces defeated only to be saved by a gringo tourist would certainly be seen as weakness. I would be the horse's ass of Latin America. Do you understand?"

"Yes. May I speak freely?"

"Of course," he replied, happy that Scott knew his place and asked for permission.

"I want nothing more to do with this. It's not my fight, it's not my business. I am glad that I was able to help, but I don't want recognition. I never have. I just want to move on. I give you my word I will speak to no one about this."

"Your word? I don't know you very well Mr. Green. What do I know about your word?"

The Dominican Republic is a place where men need to know how to keep a low profile. But it is also a place where men need to know how to stick out their chests and be macho. The difficult part is deciding when to do which. Scott looked at the president directly in the eyes.

"Actions speak louder than words. Correct?"

"Indeed they do."

"My actions earlier have enabled your words now."

They locked stares for several seconds. The president smiled and agreed.

"Indeed they have."

Scott felt the need to add to his words. "Sir, I have plans with my life that would be adversely affected by being involved in this. What about bystanders?"

"I am not worried about them. Military intelligence will issue a statement, it will not be questioned. If anyone mentions a gringo we will dismiss it as rumor. A full investigation will be warranted, but your involvement will not be needed. I am sure I know where this came from, although, there are many thugs who would benefit from my death."

The president picked up the phone and dialed an extension. "Chicho, come here please." Seconds later, the door opened and the balding man entered. The president made a formal introduction.

"This is Colonel "Chicho" Gonzalez, my chief of security and brother in law."

Brother in law? That explains a lot. "We've met," replied Scott.

The president stood and approached Scott with his hand out. "Mr. Green, Chicho will see that you get home safely and discreetly. Thank you for your help today. I am afraid I owe you a debt that I will never be able to publicly recognize or repay. But if I can ever do anything for you, do not hesitate to ask. It is a matter of honor."

They shook hands and looked each other in the eyes for several seconds. *He seems genuine. But who knows? Some of these guys are great actors.*

Chicho motioned for Scott to follow him to the back of the palace. A car was waiting for them. They drove to Scott's hotel in silence. When they arrived in the parking lot, Chicho turned around and handed Scott one of his cards. He would not make eye contact and instead looked down.

"Thank you, Mr. Green."

"Thanks for the ride."

The receptionist's smile turned to concern as Scott entered the lobby. His knees were scraped and there were dry stains of blood on both of his knees.

"I fell. I wasn't paying attention and fell. Don't worry about it."

She nodded her head as he walked past the desk and up the stairs to his room. *Crazy gringo.*

Scott took a shower and cleaned his cuts and scrapes. He was lucky. *Why did I go running into that? Why didn't I just keep going? It wasn't my fight.* He finished drying off and looked at himself in the mirror. He looked good, strong and confident. The cross around his neck was sparkling and he immediately knew why he did it. *Because it was the right thing to do.*

Scott admired the engagement ring in one hand and held the phone in the other. Esperanza sounded busy when she answered the phone at the restaurant.

"Guess who?"

"Hello handsome! How is the capital?"

"It's the same as it was before, nothing exciting to report."

"Guess what?"

"Tell me."

"The refrigerator company called me. The new motor won't be in until next week."

"Wonderful, so I'm down here for nothing?"

"Please don't be mad. I promise I'll make it up to you."

"I could never be mad at you. But I'll still let you make it up to me."

"Good. I have a surprise for you when you get back, but we're really busy right now so I have to go"

"I'm looking forward to it. I have a surprise for you too."
"I love surprises, but not as much as I love you. Please be safe."
"I always am." *Well, I usually am.*

Chapter 24

Colonial Zone
Santo Domingo

Scott woke up at 7:30AM to take another shower, pack his bag and leave. There was no hot water, but he didn't mind. The cold water would wake him up nicely for the ride north to Cabrera.

He smiled at the receptionist who could barely keep her eyes open as she checked Scott out of his room. They only accepted cash as payment, but Scott knew the drill and was prepared.

"Adios," he said, as he walked out the lobby.

"Yeah, adios." He could hear faintly from behind.

Scott opened the door to the car and reached back to unlock the rear door. He opened it and tossed his backpack onto the back seat. Out of the corner of his eye he saw a black limousine approach. He tried not to look directly at it. *Come on guys, you got my help for free. Just let me get out of here.*

"Scott Green," said a voice from behind him.

He turned to see a man standing next to the limousine and holding his sport coat to the side so Scott could see his pistol.

"Who wants to know?"

"Are you Scott Green? Someone wants to talk to you, someone very important."

"Oh yeah? Everybody's important these days," he replied, as he approached the vehicle.

"Would you get in the car please?"

"Maybe I will, maybe I won't."

The rear window of the limousine came down and Scott heard a familiar voice coming from the back seat. "Come on Scott. I'd get out of the car to talk to you, but I hate the heat down here." It was Senator Roland Burke.

Scott was stunned, but controlled his outward appearance. He approached the limousine and looked down on the Senator.

"What could you possibly want with me?"

"Get in, we'll talk about it. Scott, we're going to have this conversation one way or another. Just go with the flow, all I want to do is talk. The other door is unlocked."

Scott knew there was no way out of it. He walked around the limousine, opened the door and sat across from Senator Burke. Neither of them spoke as the vehicle pulled away from the hotel. After several minutes, Burke broke the silence.

"So what have you been doing with yourself?"

"Nothing. Vacation."

"Come on Scott. We both know you've been doing a lot more than vacation."

"You tell me then? How'd you know I was here?"

"How's the shoulder?"

"It's ok, but still sore sometimes."

"It didn't hold you back yesterday. I hear from Blaster that you were in rare form. That's why I flew in this morning to talk to you personally."

Scott froze in his seat and could not speak. *Who did he hear it from? Blaster?*

"Did you? Was Blaster part of that fiasco? I must have missed him."

"You didn't miss much else. He was in the overwatch position. It's better to use local thugs sometimes for the actual work, but they still need to be supervised. After all, they're typically not very well trained and even more undisciplined. Anyway, you seem to be in the wrong place at the wrong time a lot. But you'd never know from the newspapers."

Senator Burke threw one of the daily papers across onto Scott's lap. The front page had a large picture of the president pinning a medal on his brother in law's chest. The caption read: *Colonel "Chicho" Gonzalez accepts award for valor and courage in the face of yesterday's assassination attempt.* Scott threw the paper back and replied.

"That's fine by me."

"I though it would be. You never were big on recognition were you? But like I said, you sure seem to be in the wrong place at the wrong time a lot. That's your saving grace Scott. If I thought you were deliberately interfering in my operations I'd make you disappear."

"One of your operations?"

"Cut the kid stuff Scott. You didn't believe me at Bragg, I could see it in your eyes. Your stumbling on that stash in Afghanistan was pure luck. Blaster tried to protect it, but you had to be a hero."

"Blaster?"

"Yeah, he's one of my boys. It was a good move for him too. His family farm in Wisconsin was close to foreclosure. Now his family owns half their county and they don't even know it. Listen son, blowing one of my operations by chance is understandable, but twice is just plain destiny."

"Destiny? I don't understand."

"We were meant to work together. I could use you. Hell, I need leadership in my organization. Look at what happened yesterday, that should have been an easy in and out."

"Your organization? Drug smuggling? Is that what your organization is all about?"

"More or less, but from time to time we have to eliminate obstacles as well."

"Obstacles like the current Dominican president."

"Exactly, you're learning fast. His administration has different goals than me and my associates. Listen, that'll all work out, but right now you're probably wondering why."

"Yes, I am."

"It's pretty simple, Scott. Money beyond your wildest dreams. I'm not talking about a few million for you. I'm talking tens of millions a year. The kind of money that can make worries disappear for you and everyone you care about for the rest of eternity. Do you like to travel? Then why not pay cash for houses around the world. Do you like airplanes and boats? Then buy some. It's that easy and that's why I do it. Somebody's gonna do it and it might as well be me. I don't lose a wink of sleep over it and neither should you."

Scott was taken aback. *Neither will I? What does that mean?*

"That's a lot of money. What's the sacrifice?"

"None! What the hell do you care if junkies want to blow their brains out with dope? They're going to get it anyway, but it's going to be to someone else's benefit. If we don't benefit from the product then the terrorists or other rogue nations will. The bigger the piece of the pie we take, the less the real bad guys get. It's that simple."

"It's that simple?"

"Yes, it is. Scott, you've given your life to your country and what has it got you? It got you shot and you're almost broke. Is that the way you deserve to be treated? Because that's not how I treat my boys. They live like kings and in the grand scheme I ask for very little."

"So what do you want from me?"

"Join me. Hell, you don't even have to move. You can run my Caribbean and South American Ops from here. You've been all over this island, you must like it."

"How do you know where I've been?"

"That's the best part. I have all of the resources of the national government and especially Homeland Security at my disposal. We're wired right into the system, but we're not even there, no questions asked. We have complete anonymity and amnesty, compliments of the interests of National Security and parts of the Patriot Act. I am accountable to no one."

"So you've had me followed."

"Scott, I don't have to have people followed. I can follow you from home through phone calls, emails, banking activity, whatever. People leave trails by living, privacy is an outdated concept. But that's not the important stuff. The important stuff is for you to take some time to think seriously about improving your lifestyle. Do what you have to do. I trust you. Believe it or not I trust you."

"Why do you trust me?"

"You know what I'm capable of and won't mess with me. You'll lose and you know it. You don't have much of your own to lose, but everyone has something. But wait, Scott, that's not a threat. It's just a fact. I've liked you since the beginning. Hell, I need someone like you."

Scott stared at Burke through the entire conversation, but maintained his best poker face. He despised being threatened in any way. It didn't matter who was doing the threatening.

"Scott, you take some time to think and relax a bit. I'll be in touch and we can go from there. I know I don't have to say it, but don't do anything stupid. Ok?"

"And if I say no?"

"If you say no, you walk away no questions asked. You won't try to screw me. If you do a lot of other people will go down and I'll pin it on you. It's easily done."

"Like you did to Frances?"

Burke thought for a second. "Exactly, like I did to Frances. I almost forgot about that one."

"So, Frances was clean and Blaster and Diablo are two of your boys?"

Burke shook his head slowly, "Yes they are Scott. Yes they are. But don't hold a grudge, it will eat you up. It's much easier to just let it go."

The driver came to a slow stop and tapped on the tinted divider, signaling that they had arrived back at Scott's hotel. Body language speaks volumes. Scott made a point not to ball his hands into fists. Instead he placed them on his knees and maintained eye contact with Burke. He tried not to give away his feelings of disgust and rage.

"You can go now. I have to fly back to D.C., but I'll be in touch. And Scott, think about it. Think about what you can do with that kind of money."

Scott nodded and exited the limousine. The driver pressed the accelerator and sped away. He stood alone looking across the street at his rental car in the parking lot.

Senator Burke pressed the intercom button and spoke loudly, "Viper?"

The divider came down and his second in command turned around to face him as they spoke. "Sir?"

"What do you think?"

"I think he might go for it. Give it some time for those dollar signs to sink in."

"I don't think so. I could see it in his eyes. They were the same as at Bragg. I don't think this kid cares about money. He's all messed up in the head from growing up with no mommy and daddy. He's too short sighted to see how much good you could do with that much money, regardless of how you earn it."

"Maybe if we give him a chance he'll come around."

"Forget it. He's not going to go for it. He's a liability now."

"Sir, I think if he knew…"

Burke raised his voice. "I said he's got to go. I can't take any more chances. He keeps showing up at the worst times for me. You saved him for as long as you could, but now he has to go. Take him out immediately. I want this done ASAP."

Viper paused, then bowed his head and conceded. "Yes sir."

Scott sat in his car with his hands on the wheel looking straight forward. Thoughts flew in and out of his mind. His life had finally seemed to come together when the past came back to haunt him.

What do I do now? There's no way I'd ever join a pig like Burke, no matter how much money there is to be made. He knows I'll never do it. He could see it in my eyes.

Why has he kept me alive? Why is he giving me a chance? Blaster must have killed that poor Afghani guide. Diablo killed Frances. Why didn't they kill me? Why the offer now? Why not just kill me?

His pulse raced and the sweat poured from his brow. He felt violated. *They've tracked my every move? How much do they know? Do they know about Esperanza? She is all I have.*

Scott did not believe that this was an offer that he could walk away from. He could see it in Burke's eyes. They were the same eyes that lied to him at Fort Bragg. Burke's proposed options were to join or die. He would choose neither. Selling out and compromising all of his integrity was not an option, no matter how much money could be made. Scott had built his life around service and now he was in love for the first time. He would not betray those pure feelings for blood money. But he also wouldn't stick around to be an easy target.

Chapter 25

Cristo Rey
Santo Domingo

Scott drove the car around for several minutes, checking to see if he was being followed. He wasn't, but that didn't mean that his car wasn't bugged when he was riding around with Burke. After stopping at an ATM machine and withdrawing a large amount of cash, he continued to drive.

It was almost 9AM when he stopped the car and parked on the side of the road in the Cristo Rey sector of Santo Domingo. The barrio was absent of the beautiful and bright colors of the Colonial Zone. The atmosphere and mood resembled a depressing, black and white movie, a place of little hope.

There were many people in the streets walking back and forth as they looked curiously at Scott. It was very unusual to see a gringo tourist in the neighborhood, especially unaccompanied by a Dominican.

Scott grabbed his wallet from his front pocket and pulled out his debit card and credit cards. He then took a black pen from the glove compartment and wrote his pin numbers on the back of the cards in large block numbers. He removed the business card from his hotel and wrote his eBay and Amazon.com passwords on the back of it. After throwing the business card onto the dashboard of the car in plain view, he placed the keys on the front seat as he exited the car. He left his passport in the middle console. It was no good to him now. He knew if he wanted to live, he would have to do so under the radar.

After closing the unlocked doors of the rental car, Scott started walking towards the nearest bus station. He looked to make sure he was being watched by the locals, but not followed by professionals. He could see three local men bow their heads as they watched, but pretended not to see him drop his bank cards behind him as he walked.

Scott turned left at the next corner and entered a small store to buy a bottle of water. He placed his cell phone on the counter as he reached into his pockets to remove his money. After paying, he deliberately left the phone and continued to walk quickly towards the bus station. He turned around to check again for any followers. There were none. Burke and his boys would have a tough time tracking him now. *Please God, don't leave me. Stay with me as I know you always have.*

Chapter 26

Cabrera, Dominican Republic

Scott bought a bus ticket to Cabrera, but decided to get off in San Francisco de Macoris to stretch his legs, think and call Esperanza from a pay phone. Hector said that she was there in the morning, but left early. She seemed happy about something and had left an envelope for Scott at the bar. Scott thanked him and hung up the phone.

He looked around the main street and decided against getting back on the bus. It was slow and he hated not having control of the situation. He brainstormed about what he would do when he finally reached Esperanza. *Would she understand? Would she come with me? Where? We would be stricken to a life of complete secrecy. Maybe we could eventually get to Cuba or South America. The decision is hers. I'll understand either way. I have to get to her.*

There were several men in front of the gas station drinking beer and listening to Merengue at an earth piercing volume. There were three motorcycles in front of the pumps. Scott approached and tapped one of the men on the back to get his attention.

"Do you rent these?"

"Si, Si. How long you need it for?"

"I only need it for a couple of days. How much is it?"

"Its fifty dollars per day my friend."

Scott reached into his pocket and removed $150.

"Here, take this I'm in a hurry."

"Ok. You got a passport?"

"Not with me, it's in my hotel."

"All right no problem. Come inside and fill out some paperwork first."

Scott wrote down the name of a hotel he had seen on the way into town and scribbled a random room number next to it. No questions were asked. Ten minutes later Scott was racing north. A large red helmet covered his head and face. It was tough to see that he was a foreigner. He looked like all of the other crazy motorcyclists that dotted the landscape. He was in Cabrera in under an hour and went directly to the restaurant.

Hector saw Scott enter the restaurant so he retrieved Esperanza's note from behind the bar and handed it to him.

"Here you go, Scott."

"Thanks Hector. Is everything ok?"

"Of course, why wouldn't it be?"

"I'm just asking."

Scott opened the sealed envelope and read the note.

Hi Handsome,

I got a good deal on a beach house for the next few days and I'm taking some time off from work. The refrigerator is down and so is business. Nobody knows where we are and there will be no distractions. I already did the grocery shopping and packed some of your things from the apartment (I hope you don't mind). All I need now is you, so follow the enclosed map to find me when you get back. And remember Shhhh-hhh...don't tell anybody where we are.

Loving you and waiting,

Esperanza

His heart warmed and some of his anxiety was relieved. It was as if she had read his mind. The arrangements wouldn't do for long, but it was a start. It would be good enough for at least a day or two. He had a lot of explaining to do. *Will she understand that this isn't my fault or my plan? Am I asking for too much?*

What would I do if the situation was reversed? He looked at the map, committed it to memory and waved to Hector on his way out.

It took twenty five minutes to reach the house after stopping several times to make sure he wasn't being followed. The long, gravel driveway twisted and turned up a hill before straightening and leveling off at the main entrance of the house. Scott could not see any activity as he removed his helmet, placed it on the seat of the motorcycle, and combed his hair with his hands.

The two story house was beautiful and the location was secluded. Scott opened the front door and entered without announcing his arrival. He could smell something cooking in the kitchen, but could not quite place it. He walked slowly around the ground floor, making note of the house layout. After doing the same on the upstairs level he started to get nervous. *Where is she? This food isn't cooking itself. God, I hope I have the right house.*

Scott approached the sliding glass door at the back of the house, it was half open. He exhaled deeply when he saw Esperanza sitting in a chair reading about fifty feet away. She sat on a small terrace overlooking the water. The cool water of the Atlantic crashed on the rocks below. The scene was tranquil and beautiful, just like her.

He did not want to startle her, so he spoke as he walked across the back lawn towards the terrace. "Hello there."

She turned her head to look and bounced out of her seat. "Hey! I'm out here. I thought you'd never make it."

"Of course I'm here," he said, as they kissed and embraced firmly.

She looked into his eyes. "What's wrong?"

"Nothing is wrong. I'm just glad to see you." He knew that things would never be the same after the conversation that they had to have and decided that it could wait.

"I'm glad to see you too. What do you think? Isn't it great? It's totally private and nobody knows we're here. It's just you and me."

"And that's exactly what we need right now."

"Yes it is. We definitely need some time alone," she said, as she squeezed him again and held him tight. "Let's have a glass of wine."

Esperanza led him into the house by the hand and went into the kitchen to check on dinner. "I'm cooking a traditional Dominican dinner for you tonight."

Scott locked the front door and surveyed the area again as he replied. "That sounds good. I'm starving."

"Can you come in here and open the wine? What are you doing?"

"Nothing, I'm just looking around. This is a great house. Who knows we're here?"

"I told you, nobody. I rented it from a woman who I know from Puerta Plata. I paid her cash for 3 days and she hopped on a plane to Spain for a week. If we decide to stay longer, we can work it out with her when she returns."

"Good."

"Yes it is. No distractions."

They opened the sliding glass doors all the way and sat at the kitchen table for hours eating and talking. Esperanza did most of the talking as Scott stared across the table into her eyes. None of the subjects discussed were of any particular importance, but Scott hung on her every word. He was entirely captivated by her, but nervous about their future.

How can I expect her to come with me? How can I ask her to do that? I love her. I cannot imagine life without her, she is the only reason I'm alive. But my love for her is my liability. It's the only way to get at me. If Burke knows about her or learns about us, he'll have a way to get at me. I don't care about myself, but I cannot bare the thought of anyone hurting her. I have to protect her at all costs. She's in danger by knowing me. I'm so sorry I dragged you into this. Will you understand?

"What are you staring at me for? Will you say something? Or am I doing enough talking for the both of us?" She laughed and smiled widely.

Scott returned the smile and put his hand on hers. "Not at all, I love listening to you talk. And I love seeing you smile and laugh. It reminds me of all the good in the world."

"I love you," she said.

They spent the early evening on the terrace overlooking the ocean and barely speaking. She lay on Scott's lap with her arms wrapped around his neck. The waves pounded against the rocks and the cool breeze offered relief from the humidity.

"Honey, we need to talk about some things, some very important things."

"Ok," she answered, without looking up, resting her head against Scott's chest.

"I have been thinking a lot lately and I want you to know how much I love you. I also want you to know that there is absolutely no doubt in my mind that I want to spend the rest of my life with you."

She sat up and looked into his eyes. A smile spread across her face and tears formed in the corners of her charcoal eyes. "I love you too. You know that don't you?"

"Yes. But we're going to have some very real challenges. This will not be easy, for reasons that you need to know in advance. And if you don't want to continue I would understand completely."

"Stop it! Stop right there. Wasn't it me who taught you everything happens for a reason? God brought us together, Scott. Only he can separate us. I know that you have had some tough times in your life and your career. But those things are what have defined you and made you into the man I love. I wouldn't change any of them even if I could. Everything happens for a reason."

"You don't understand. My past could present some dangers for us in the future because…"

"Listen to me. There is nothing you could say to me that would change my mind about you. Whatever you want to tell me can wait until tomorrow. Ok? Can we just have tonight without any distractions or problems? Let's make tonight a perfect night."

Scott looked at her and nodded his head, it could wait until tomorrow and so could the ring. Right now everything was perfect. She pressed her lips against his and kissed him more passionately than she ever had. He caressed her neck and held her tightly, wishing that the moment would last forever, but knowing it wouldn't.

"Take me inside, I've waited my entire life for this night." she said.

Scott picked her up and carried her through the sliding glass doors and into the house. There were no lights, so he put her down and turned on the small light above the kitchen sink.

"Why don't you go upstairs and get into your pajamas? I'll lock up down here and straighten things up a bit."

"Ok," she said, as she kissed him softly on the cheek.

He watched her climb the stairs and then went around the ground floor locking all of the doors and windows. She yelled down the stairs to him.

"Do you want to go to the beach tomorrow or just relax here at the house?"

"Anything you want to do is fine by me?"

"No really, which do you prefer?"

"As long as I'm with you I don't care."

"Good answer," she chuckled, as she turned on the shower. "Hey, did you get my email?"

"Huh? What do you mean?"

"I wasn't sure if you would call me from the Capital so I sent you an email to say good night, sweet dreams, that kind of stuff. I thought maybe you'd be checking it."

Scott froze and recalled the words of Senator Burke. *"Phone calls, emails, banking activity, whatever."* His mind started racing and instinct took over.

"Where did you send me that email from?"

"I don't know, yesterday afternoon I think."

Scott raised his voice, his concern was obvious. "No, where did you send it from?"

"I sent it from the den downstairs. It has a cable modem connection. You know that's much faster than that dial up connection I have at home. I'm going to look into getting it."

Scott immediately knew that their location was compromised. His pulse sky rocketed as he started to climb the stairs and yell. "Esperanza, turn off the light!"

"What? Why? I'm about to take a shower."

He reached the landing of the staircase and turned right to climb the final flight when he yelled again. "Turn off the light right now!"

He reached the top of the stairs and sprinted down the long hallway to the master bedroom. As he crossed through the threshold he saw Esperanza standing in the middle of the room looking at him curiously.

"What?" she asked.

Scott slammed his hand against the light switch on the wall next to the door and the room went dark. One second later he heard a popping sound followed by small pieces of glass shattering on the tile floor.

The bullet ripped through her head in a split second. The only saving grace of her death was that she died almost instantly. The shooter was either very well trained or very lucky. Either way, she died right in front of him. Within seconds her clothes were crimson. Everything else in his life never seemed to turn out the way it was supposed to. This was no exception. Before he could even think about crying or mourning, before he could go to her to touch her just one more time, he felt his heart harden as his emotional wall rebuilt itself.

As the blood started to spill from her lifeless body, he began mentally preparing himself for what he knew she would disapprove of, but what he felt that he must do. She would be avenged.

He stared at her for several seconds before being distracted by the sound of the front door being forced open. The killer was coming to check on his target. Scott quickly and quietly walked down the hallway and crouched at the top of the stairs. There was no time to grab anything to use as a weapon. He would have to do this the old fashioned way.

The killer silently climbed the stairs, pausing briefly on the landing, before continuing. Before he could reach the top, Scott stood up and kicked him full force in the face. The pistol in his hand flew into the air as he fell backwards, landing on the rifle that was slung across his back. Before he knew what happened, Scott grabbed him by the shirt and threw him down the remaining flight of stairs.

The killer tried desperately to get to his feet and defend himself, but Scott was filled with uncontrollable rage and pounded him relentlessly with punches to the head and midsection. He stumbled backwards as Scott advanced and kicked him square in the chest causing him to fly backwards through the closed sliding glass door. The sound of shattering glass filled the night air.

Scott kicked him until he was clear of the pile of broken glass and then pounced on top of him. The man was bloody from head to toe, but Scott could see his face clearly in the moonlight. It was Blaster.

"You bastard," Scott said, as he raised his fist to deliver yet another blow to Blaster's head.

His eyes glanced down and saw the shimmer of a metal blade. Blaster had drawn a knife from his belt and tried to stab Scott in the abdomen. Scott blocked with his left hand and connected with a punch to the head with his right. Blaster managed to squirm out of the way and kick Scott off of him. He stumbled to his feet and retreated onto the lawn, his knife at the ready.

"Hey Scotty, I guess I missed you and for that I am truly sorry. Getting shot would have been a lot less painful than this is going to be."

"You have no idea what you've done, but you're going to pay for it anyway."

Blaster lunged at Scott with the knife, but he was able to side step and trap Blaster's wrist. Scott bent the knife upwards and held it against Blaster's throat. They both struggled for control as Scott pushed Blaster back towards the cliff.

"Come on, you can do better than this."

Scott stared into his eyes and with all of his might pushed on the knife. The blade made no sound when it cut into Blaster's throat, but Scott could hear the blood as it began to spray. He grabbed Blaster firmly by the shirt, spun him around and threw him off of the cliff. The fall was silent, but Scott could hear the body as it landed on the jagged rocks below. He fell to his knees to catch his breath.

The house was dark and completely silent. Scott sat for several minutes listening for any sign that Blaster may not have been alone. He could hear little besides the pounding of his heart and the surf on the rocks below. Scott looked up at the house and tried not to think about Esperanza's lifeless body on the floor upstairs.

After quietly entering the house, he knelt next to her body and looked down at her. He was unable to cry, numbness took over and he felt paralyzed. After several minutes he lifted her gently and carried her slowly to the bed. He placed her in the center and sat in a chair in the corner of the room looking at her. *I killed her. I killed her by saving her. I should have ended it all on the roof of my apartment. They might have killed her, but I wouldn't have been responsible. And I wouldn't be here now. I would rather be dead. Love equals loss. I should have known better.*

He sat in the chair staring at her until the sun started to rise. Then he got up and sat next to her on the bed. Her hair was soft and smooth as he stroked it and touched her face with his hands. He crossed her arms in front of her and knelt at the foot of the bed. Her meticulously painted toes felt cold when he placed his hands on them and rested his head on his hands to pray for the last time.

Revenge. Burke would pay for this. He would pay for this if it was to be Scott's final mission in life. The odds were against his success and he accepted the fact that he would probably die in the process, but it had to be done. Esperanza would have never approved. *I'm sorry, my love.*

Scott stood up, reached into his pocket and removed the ring. He knelt next to her and slipped in onto her finger. He kissed it and spoke out loud. "I'll love you forever, you were my hope." He then leaned over her body and kissed her gently on the lips. She was cold.

Scott grabbed Esperanza's cell phone as he left the house and kick started the motorcycle. He headed south and did not stop until he needed gas. The small service station offered shade and a few minutes to finalize his plan. After paying the attendant, Scott called directory assistance for Washington D.C. A few moments later the phone was ringing as he waited for an answer. A young woman answered the phone energetically.

"Senator Burke's office, may I help you?"

Scott paused and closed his eyes before he spoke. "Yes, may I speak with Senator Burke please?"

She responded with the standard answer. "I'm sorry, but he isn't available right now. May I take a message and he or a member of his staff will return your call?"

"No. Tell him Scott Green is on the phone. I'm sure he'll take the call."

"Sir, Senator Burke is very busy right now and…"

"Just tell him please. I'm sure he'd want to know if I was calling."

"Ok. I'll let him know. Hold please."

Thirty seconds later Scott heard the Senator's voice on the other end of the line.

"Green?"

"Yes, does that surprise you?"

"Why would it surprise me?"

"Because you just tried to have me killed."

There was a pause on the line. Then he replied, "Yes I did and that's something I personally wanted to do a long time ago, but was persuaded not to. Where's Blaster?"

"He's dead, but you two will be reunited soon enough. I promise you that."

"Really? You sound pretty confident."

"You killed the only woman I've ever loved. You'll be dead soon. And I just wanted you to know that I'm the one who's going to do it. You took the only thing I had in my life. Now you have to pay."

"Do you think I actually care about your little whore? You listen to me you arrogant little bastard. You have no idea what you're up against. Do you hear me? Green? Green?"

The line was dead. Senator Burke immediately dialed his secretary's extension and started speaking before she could answer. "Get me Barnes at the TTC immediately." He removed his oversized Mont Blanc pen from his shirt pocket and tapped it on his mahogany desk as he waited.

"This is Barnes."

"Barnes, this is Senator Burke? Are you at the TTC?"

"No sir, I'm at lunch with a friend right now."

"Well, you need to get your ass back there immediately and get me an update on Scott Green, codename Xpatriot. I want you to make him your number one priority. Got it?"

"Yes. I'll finish my lunch and head back right away."

"Take your lunch with you. I need this information now. It's a matter of national security." His words were followed by a dial tone.

Barnes got excited by the words 'national security' and the fact that he had anything to do with them. He looked across the table at his lunch date that he had met on the internet and spoke proudly.

"I wish I could tell you what that was about, but it's highly classified."

"For real?" she asked, as she chewed her gum with her mouth open. "So you work for the government or something? That's exciting!"

"You have no idea, baby. But for now I have to go. I'm sorry I can't explain more. I'll call you." He stood and walked quickly out of the diner. She felt exhilarated and excited until the waitress brought her the check.

Chapter 27

Presidential Palace
Santo Domingo

Scott was almost out of gas by the time he reached the gates of the Presidential Palace in Santo Domingo. He parked to the side of the guard shack and knocked on the glass door. Two armed guards came out to see what the gringo wanted.

"I need to speak to Colonel Gonzalez."

"Who are you? Why do you need to see Colonel Chicho? He is a very important man. Does he know you?"

Scott removed the Colonel's card from his pocket and replied. "Yes, he knows me. Tell him Scott Green is here and it's very important."

The guards looked at each other and nodded. One of the men entered the shack and picked up the phone. Five minutes later he was leading Scott down the hallway of the main floor of the palace towards the Colonel's office.

Chicho was waiting in the doorway and spoke first. "Mr. Green, I didn't think I would be seeing you so soon."

"Me neither," replied Scott, as Chicho shut the door behind him. "I need to speak to the president."

"You do?"

"Yes, I do. I have information about his assassination attempt yesterday and I need to speak with him ASAP."

"Mr. Green, your assistance is no longer needed. We are in full control of the situation."

"I know. I saw your picture in the paper. Congratulations. Now are you going to let me speak to the president or do you want me to walk out the front steps of the palace and straight to the newspapers?"

Chicho was not accustomed to being spoken like a common soldier. But after considering the potential humiliation of the truth made public he conceded.

"There is no need to make threats."

"I don't like making them. But believe me, this is important. And it's the least you can do for me. Is he here?"

"Yes, but he is leaving tomorrow for his annual state visit to Spain."

"I know and I have to see him before he goes."

"Very well, wait here."

Chicho left the office and shut the door behind him. Scott glanced at the awards and citations that covered his office walls and shook his head. *I wonder what he didn't do for these.* Chicho returned in less than five minutes and led Scott to the president's office through a series of back corridors.

"And you are positive that this man is responsible for yesterday's attack?"

"Yes sir, without a doubt. I have told you everything. You and I are the only two people with this information. I have lost the only thing I had to live for. You lost ten of your men and almost your life. I am asking this favor of you both as repayment for my assistance and so I can avenge both of our losses. As you said before, it is a matter of honor."

Scott had spent the last thirty minutes telling the president everything. He started with Afghanistan, explained his conversation with Burke and ended with the death of Esperanza. The president stared at Scott's eyes and asked no questions until he was finished.

"I am sorry. The loss of a woman in such a barbaric manner hurts all of mankind."

"Yes, it does."

"I spent the morning with my grieving sister. Her only two sons were members of my security detail, both were killed in the attack. It pains me more than you know to see her cry."

"Then help me, sir. Help me avenge them all. It is the only way. The players in this game are too powerful to battle within the system. I'll cut off the head of the snake or die trying."

"Are you prepared for such a fate?"

"Yes. I have no reservations. But if you help me, my chances of taking him out are much better. Also, I know I'm asking a lot and that this could come back to you and damage your relationship with the U.S."

"The interests of the Dominican people come first for me, not the U.S. And my confidence in the current American administration has been waning for some time, especially when it comes to investigating their own corruption. I believe Winston Churchill was right when he said that countries do not have friends, they have interests." The president lit a cigarette, inhaled deeply and looked at the ceiling as he exhaled. "You are asking for a lot, but you have done much for me. I will do it, but I want you to promise me something."

"Anything," Scott replied.

"Promise me you will do all you can to destroy this pig. Do it for your friend, your wife and the sons of my sister. Do it for us all."

Scott winced when the president referred to Esperanza as his wife, but quickly recovered and strengthened the wall. "Sir, I promise you that he will pay."

"Then I will see that she is given a proper and respectful burial. As for your other requests, we had better get started. We have much to do and very little time."

Chapter 28

▼

Terrorist Tracking Center (TTC) Richmond, Virginia

Smitty was reading a website about alien autopsy results when he heard Barnes scurry through the security door. He minimized the site he was reading and popped up an Arabic news site before Barnes was close enough to see what he was doing.

"I need a situation report on the Xpatriot file ASAP. I don't care what you're doing, just get the information now."

"I'm fine and you? Thanks. Yeah, it's good to see you too."

"Not now Smitty, this is our chance to impress the big boys. Have you been keeping an eye on this guy?" Barnes was breathing heavily; he had been running since leaving his car in the secure lot.

"Give me five minutes and I'll have a full report for you."

"Ok. I'll be in my office. Call me as soon as you have anything."

"I will."

Chapter 29

Washington D.C.
United States

At 6PM eastern time the presidential airplane of the Dominican Republic landed at Reagan International Airport, Washington D.C. An official from the U.S. Department of State was waiting on the ground to receive the deplaning diplomats, a courtesy extended to dignitaries and foreign diplomats. A car from the Dominican embassy was waiting as well.

The president's personal attaché deplaned first and explained to the State Department representative that only one diplomat would be staying, the rest of the passengers were bound for Madrid.

"Oh Madrid, I wish I could go with you," she said with a smile.

"And we wish you could come."

They talked about small things until a man appeared in the door of the plane and walked confidently down the stairs. He smiled at the American as he held out his diplomatic credentials before being asked.

The agent held the identification up and matched the pictures. "Welcome to the United States Señor Verde. Enjoy your stay."

"Muchas gracias, I'm sure I will," replied Scott Green.

Chapter 30

Terrorist Tracking Center (TTC) Richmond, Virginia

"This is Barnes."

"You might want to get out here. I have the Xpatriot file updated."

"Anything interesting?"

"You need to see this."

Barnes hung up the phone and ran into the operations center. Smitty was standing in front of his monitor with papers and pictures scattered on the table in front of him. He began talking as soon as Barnes arrived.

"Ok, here's the deal. This guy has been pretty active. He's spending money like a madman. $3,000 on eBay yesterday, another $1,000 on Amazon.com today, but get this, he's delivering the stuff all over the world. Most of it is going to an address in the Washington Heights section of New York City, some to another address in San Juan and a few things to Zurich. He has also made calls to at least three different countries in Europe."

"So what? You called me in here to tell me he's shopping?"

"No. He's also been pulling money out of ATMs. But one withdrawal was in Santo Domingo and there was another ten minutes later in Santiago."

"So what does that mean?"

"Santiago is a two or three hour drive. He couldn't have done them both. So, I downloaded the photos from both and it's just as I expected. They were two different people." Smitty held up two 8x10 photos, both of different men.

"Ok, so what?"

"I think somehow he knew we were tracking him so he's trying to throw us off his trail. But, I checked INTERPOL for passport activity. He departed Santo Domingo and is on a flight to Brazil as we speak. I tried to get a picture from the airport, but Santo Domingo is behind the times and isn't totally wired yet. He lands in Rio de Janeiro within the next two hours and I can get a digital picture the second he steps off the plane and tries to get through immigration."

"Ok. Ok. Good job Smitty. I'll pass this along. Good stuff, foolproof. You can run, but you can't hide. This guy's biggest mistake was thinking he was smarter than me."

"Yeah, big mistake," Smitty said, as he rolled his eyes and sat down.

Chapter 31

Reagan International Airport Washington D.C.

Scott asked the driver if he could borrow his cell phone and to turn down the radio so he could make a call. *I never knew there were merengue stations in D.C.*

Scott called Senator Burke's office, the secretary answered after the third ring.

"Yes, this is William Gamble with the Washington Post. May I speak with the Senator please?"

"I'm sorry Senator Burke is not available, but if you leave a message he or a staff member will return your call."

"Oh, I'm sorry. I didn't realize he was out of town."

"He's in town, but very busy and will be in meetings all night. May I take a message?"

"No that's ok. He asked me to call him, but you said he'll be busy tonight. Would it be better if I called back in the morning?"

"Yes. I would imagine he'll be in meetings until at least ten tonight, but if you'd like to call back tomorrow he may have some time. Hello? Hello?" The line was dead.

Chapter 32

Capitol Building Washington D.C.

Senator Burke was sitting behind his large mahogany desk, listening with the phone to his ear. Barnes filled him in on the Xpatriot's movements over the past 24 hours.

"Ok. And you think he's on this plane to Brazil?"

"Absolutely. Don't worry. I'm always a step ahead of these guys. They try, but when it comes down to it, they're just not smart enough to fool me."

"I see. Call me as soon as you have something."

Senator Burke hung up the phone and looked at Viper. "They think he's on his way to Brazil. He's running."

"Do they have a positive ID? Scott's not the running type."

"Close enough. Besides, this net doesn't have any holes in it. I gave INTERPOL instructions to detain him. It's just a matter of time before he pops up somewhere."

Scott told the driver to forget about parking and drop him off in front of the Capital building. As the car slowed to a stop, he looked out the window, breathed deeply and exhaled.

"Do you want me to wait or come back for you?"

"That won't be necessary. Thanks for the ride."

"Yes sir."

Scott closed the car door and listened as the driver turned up the radio and drove away. The sounds of Dominican music could be heard through the closed doors and windows.

This would be Scott's first time in the Capitol building. He wished it were under different circumstances, but that was out of his control. Everything had been set into motion by Diablo and destiny had brought him here. *Everything happens for a reason.* When he reached the top of the stairs, he entered the building and approached the security checkpoint.

A security guard approached him. "Sorry, but visiting hours for the public ended at five."

"I'm not the public. I have business here." Scott replied, as he removed his diplomatic passport.

"Pardon me, Sir, I'm sorry. Right this way."

The guard glanced at the picture on the ID and motioned for Scott to walk through the metal detector. The security personnel were courteous and respectful. Scott wondered if that was standard or because he was a dignitary. He approached one of the guards.

"Can you tell me where I can find Senator Roland Burke's office?"

"There is a directory straight ahead. It should be self explanatory, but let me know if you need any help."

"Thank you."

Chapter 33

▼

Terrorist Tracking Center (TTC) Richmond, Virginia

Smitty finished reading about the latest UFO cover up conspiracies and looked at his watch. The Xpatriot's plane was supposed to land in Rio de Janeiro fifteen minutes prior.

Ok. Ok. Ok Let's see here…flight 2701 is confirmed on the ground…early too…he must be happy about that…immigration files…ok…he's been flagged so they should have grabbed him…did they?…did they?…come on…this is soooo slow…yes!…they did…ok then, retrieve the picture from INTERPOL…come on…load…load.

"Oh God," he said out loud. *That's not Scott Green. Someone's traveling on his passport. How the hell did Santo Domingo miss that? It doesn't even look like him. This guy is black.*

Smitty picked up the phone and dialed Barnes' extension. "Houston, we have a problem."

Chapter 34

▼

Capitol Building
Washington D.C.

The security guard posted in front of Senator Burke's office held out his hand to stop Scott when he tried to casually walk past him and into the office.

"Can I help you, sir?"

"Yes, I'm here to see Senator Burke."

"Do you have an appointment? Is the secretary expecting you?"

"Yes," Scott replied confidently.

"May I have your name please?"

Scott exhaled and looked down. "I'm sorry."

"Excuse me?"

"I said I'm sorry," he answered, as he slammed the guard back against the wall and grabbed the pepper spray from his belt. Scott gave him two quick sprays in the eyes and then handcuffed the guard behind his back with his own cuffs before wrestling him into the office and pushing him onto a large sofa in the waiting area. He accidentally inhaled some of the spray and started to cough. The secretary stood up and was about to scream for help when Scott spoke.

"Shut up and get out of here. Just go."

She ran out of the office and Scott wanted to take the officer's gun, but he was instinctively clutching it with both hands and Scott didn't want to risk a misfire and injuring the man. The office was too small for the pepper spray. He would have to make due with anything he could find. He looked on the secretary's desk and grabbed her letter opener.

Scott slammed the main door to the office closed and pushed a large upholstered chair in front of it. It would not hold for long, but it would give him some time before security gets there. Surely he had been seen disarming the guard by the security cameras.

The door to the Senator's office was to the left of the secretary's desk. He pulled off his suit jacket and tie and dropped them to the floor. He twisted the knob and threw the door open. Senator Burke was sitting behind his desk. Burke was stunned and did not move or speak until after Scott had shut and locked the door behind him.

Scott approached and Burke tried to stand up to defend himself. He was met by a kick to the midsection and an uppercut that forced him back into his seat. Blood started trickling from the Senator's mouth.

"It's time to pay," Scott said. He was holding Burke's hair with his left hand and held the letter opener against his throat with the right. He pressed the opener against Burke's neck until it pierced the skin and started drawing small drops of blood.

"I told you that I was going to do it. You didn't believe me did you? Did you?"

"Viper! Viper!"

Scott did not understand what he was saying and ignored him. "Why Burke? Why did you do it? Why couldn't you just leave me alone?"

"Help!"

"Nobody can help you now. You have to pay. You're responsible for Frances and you took from me the only thing I had in my life. You sent one of my own men to kill me. I want to hear you say it. You're responsible aren't you? Aren't you? You bastard!"

"Viper! Viper!"

Scott pushed the letter opener deeper into his neck. "Say it! Say it!"

The room was dark. The only light on was the Senator's desk lamp. Scott had not noticed the figure standing in the corner when he entered the office. He could now see the man advance, his outstretched arm holding a pistol. Scott recognized the voice as soon as he heard it.

"He didn't send him, Scott. I did."

No. Scott did not want to turn and look. He did not want to verify what he already knew. Scott could recognize that voice anywhere. It was the voice of LTC McCallister.

"Back away from the Senator and drop it. Do it now, son."

Scott dropped the opener on the desk and backed away from the Senator slowly. Burke immediately reached into his jacket and removed a handkerchief to press against his neck. He stood up and ran around the opposite side of the desk to stand next to McCallister.

"Why did you wait so long? He could have killed me?"

"He didn't," McCallister replied, without taking his eyes off of Scott.

Scott had a blank expression on his face. Never, in his wildest of dreams, would he ever have thought ill of his mentor. He had been under McCallister's wing for the better part of ten years. He didn't know what to think and knew that his questions could never be answered to his satisfaction.

"Why? How could you do this? How could you sell out to a pig like him?"

"Viper, cut the chit chat and kill him now!" said Burke.

McCallister ignored Burke and replied. "It's complicated Scott. Suffice it to say that I deserved a hell of a lot more than I was getting."

"You were a respected commander of the world's greatest soldiers, the good guys, doing good work. What more could you want?"

"I want recognition! God Dammit! Recognition! Do you know how many of my West Point classmates have been promoted ahead of me? Do you? Some of them are full colonels and two are wearing stars on their shoulders! I've been busting my ass for over twenty years and what has it got me? I've been passed over for promotion and could barely afford to send my kids to college. Can you even imagine that? Twenty years of blood and sweat and nothing to show for it. Maybe that's ok for the others, but I'll pass, thank you very much. I'm better than that."

Scott let it all sink in and said nothing.

"Oh, you have nothing to say to me? Then you're just like them Scott. A little appreciation from you wouldn't hurt either."

"You want appreciation from me?" Scott asked.

"Yes I do. You owe me everything. You never would have made it into the Special Forces if I hadn't pulled for you. Hell, I saved you life in Afghanistan. I was there. Do you think Diablo let you live because he's a nice guy? I walked into that barn when he was about to cap you. Burke wanted you dead months ago, but I pulled for you. I want some appreciation! You owe me everything!"

Scott stood motionless, his eyes fixed on McCallister.

"Viper, kill him now," pleaded Burke.

Scott spoke. "And then you ordered one of my men to kill me. Instead, he killed the only woman I have ever loved. You took everything from me."

"Yeah well, things happen. And everything happens for a reason, Scott."

Burke had heard enough and tried to take the pistol from McCallister. The colonel turned and resisted. The scuffle lasted several seconds before the pistol discharged and Senator Burke fell to the ground. Blood spilled from his chest.

Scott took advantage and lunged towards McCallister, kicked the pistol out of his hand and punched him as hard as he could in the side of the head. McCallister stumbled and threw several ineffective punches of his own. Scott ducked to avoid them and picked McCallister up by the waist and slammed him down on Burke's desk with all of his might.

McCallister's head slammed against the mahogany and dazed him long enough for Scott to climb on top of him with the letter opener in his hand. He squeezed McCallister's throat with his other hand. The colonel struggled unsuccessfully. Scott's grip was tight and motivated by rage. McCallister only managed to rip open Scott's shirt, exposing the gold cross he wore around his neck.

With one flick of the wrist, Scott could accomplish his quest for revenge. He was watching the tip of the opener as he pressed it harder and harder against McCallister's neck. He rotated his eyes back and forth between the colonel's neck and eyes. He couldn't do it. He was restraining himself and didn't know why. He tried, but could not cut his throat. It was as if an invisible force had paralyzed him. And then he saw it.

He looked deep into the colonel's eyes and saw the reflection of his gold cross in them. It hung freely as Scott leaned over him. The reflection maintained Scott's attention as he remembered Esperanza's voice.

"Is that our decision to make? Who lives and who dies? The cycle continued, but I could have stopped it. I love you, Scott and God is always with you. If you ever doubt either, just look down."

The words continued to echo in his head as the door burst open and six or seven SWAT looking personnel stormed the office. Scott felt their presence, but could not hear anything until the leader spoke.

"Get off of him. Get off of him. We need him alive."

Scott did not move and continued staring at the reflection in McCallister's eyes.

"Get off of him. Back away," he repeated, as a plain clothes man entered the office behind him and spoke softly.

The plain clothes man spoke. "Scott, back off. We know everything about these guys. My name is John Delaney. I'm with the NSA. You've got to trust me on this. If you kill him, you'll go down. If you back off, everything will be fine. We know you're clean."

Scott did not respond.

"We know Frances was clean too. And we can clear his name, but you have to back away. I know how you feel, but you have to do it."

Scott shook his head back and forth to regain his senses and looked at Delaney. "If you knew, why didn't you stop them?"

"It's complicated Scott, but you have to trust me. We have more video and audio tape on these guys to put them away for a long, long time. But you have to help me out here and back away. He has information that we need. If you waste him it will do more damage than good. Ok?"

Scott thought to himself. *I know you're here with me Esperanza. Talk to me. Talk to me.* He looked down at McCallister. *The cycle ends right here.* Scott threw the letter opener onto the floor, hopped off the desk and raised his hands over his head.

"You'd better not be lying to me."

Chapter 35

National Security Agency Safe House Classified Location Washington D.C.

The next several days were spent in a safe house on the outskirts of Washington. It was a three story townhouse and was occupied by operatives twenty four hours a day. Scott told his story at least a dozen times to several different agents of varying levels. He was consistent and honest. When one agent suggested a polygraph, John Delaney shot the idea down as insulting to someone of Scott's obvious integrity. He also felt that it could turn Scott against them and hamper their ongoing investigation. They needed him.

The accommodations were good and everyone who he interacted with was respectful and sympathetic to his losses. Regardless, he could not help but drift off occasionally. The past few months had taken him from the lowest of lows to the most fulfilled he had ever been in his life. And then back down again.

Scott stood in the parlor of the townhouse looking out the window at the pedestrians walking back and forth when Delaney entered the room.

"Scott, I'm sure you'll be happy to know that we're finished for now."

"What do you mean for now?"

"Well, we may need more depositions in the future, but we have all we need for now."

"So it may never be over?"

"Probably not. But I need to speak to you about a different matter now."

Scott turned to face Delaney, but said nothing. He had eaten very little over the past week and had lost considerable weight. He felt thin, physically and emotionally.

"Scott, we need you."

"What do you mean?"

"We need you on the team. We've been gathering information on these guys for the past year and have enough to take down a lot of them, but a few have slipped through the cracks. Take a look at this picture. Do you recognize this man?"

Delaney opened a file and placed it on the table in front of Scott. The 8x10 photo was of two men sitting in a café. One had his legs crossed, a bottle of beer sat on the small table in front of him. It was Diablo. He did not recognize the other man, but he was clearly a Middle Easterner. Scott's felt his heart skip a beat as he picked up the picture to look closer.

"Yeah, that's Diablo, but I don't know the other guy. Listen, I've been doing the talking for three days, what can you tell me about him?"

"That's the problem. He's one of the big fish who got away. We were first made aware of his involvement on Burke's team when he was fingered by one of our Middle Eastern assets. It took us by surprise. He's been funneling money to terrorist organizations for God knows how long. Burke made sure his boys made money, but he didn't care where it went."

"What else do you know?"

"Scott, this is all classified. So I need your word that..."

Scott interrupted him, "Don't insult me."

"I'm sorry," Delaney said, pausing before he continued. "His real name is Juan Carlos Garcia. He was born in Miami, father was Syrian and his mother was Cuban. Diablo grew up and was educated entirely in the U.S. just like any other American kid, with one exception. He has known his Islamic mission his entire life. He's the first of what we're calling "Jihad Babies", born and bred in the U.S. to further the cause of radical Islam. God only knows how many others there are. These people have been fighting for a thousand years. Patience is one of their virtues.

"Anyway, he was indoctrinated at an early age to extremist ideologies, assimilated into the American system and then put to work. He managed to work his way into the intelligence community and even broke into Burke's rogue element before he was identified. We estimate that he has been able to funnel tens of millions of dollars to terrorist organizations all over the world. The information that he has been able to pass along can't be quantified. We also know that he was instrumental in helping some of the September 11th hijackers procure their visas."

"He sounds like someone you'd want to catch. Why don't you just track him like you did me?"

"It's not that easy. He knows our procedures and he knows how to avoid them. I'm sure he already knows about Burke and McCallister. This picture was taken yesterday in Venezuela. The other man is Abdul Allawi, in charge of Al Quaeda's South American and Caribbean operations."

"Why are they in Venezuela? Why not Syria?"

"Good question. Historically, Latin America has been in perpetual development. Many of those governments know that the U.S. and Europe have about had it with giving them aid and seeing no progress. So the Arabs enter the scene and some of the governments are more than happy to accept their drug and oil money. In exchange, the terrorists are harbored. Did you know that the largest Muslim Mosque in the southern hemisphere is in Caracas?"

"No, I didn't know that."

"Well, that's what's happening. And it gives them a closer base from which to launch their operations. Scott, we have to find him and bring him in."

"Good luck."

"Join us. We need you on the team."

Scott looked at Delaney and laughed. "In the past few months I've seen my mentor, fellow troopers and a senior Senator show me their true colors. What makes your team so different?"

"Scott, this isn't a simple operation. We're in the middle of world war three here. It all comes down to religion. They hate us because of our roots and faith, not because of our policies. It's our culture that they hate. We're not a Muslim nation and never will be. So this will never end. We need people like you, people who have faith and integrity and answer to a higher authority and won't sell out for a few bucks. I think you understand that this is a crusade. They don't despise our policies, they despise our existence. You know exactly what I mean."

"What do you know about me? You don't know me."

"I think I do. I saw you Scott. I saw you over McCallister. You could have killed him but you didn't. Why? Listen, I'm a firm believer that everything happens for a reason. The fact that you actually made it to D.C. flies in the face of logic, but you made it happen. And it happened for a reason. You could walk away right now with no questions asked, but I don't think you will."

"Why not?"

"Because you know if you did, you'd never forgive yourself. It's in your blood Scott, help us."

Scott turned away and looked out the window. People were walking and talking. Children skipped and chased each other on their way home from school, oblivious to the threats that live among them. *I could walk away. I could just walk away. But what would I do then? One day I would turn on the television, see a tragedy and wonder if I could have stopped it. What would Esperanza want me to do?* Scott closed his eyes and searched for an answer.

"Scott, we need you. What's it going to be?"

Chapter 36

Cabrera, Dominican Republic

Hector stopped the car and pointed to the first row of headstones on the right. "She is resting at the end of this row."

Scott got out of the car and retrieved the bouquet of flowers from the back seat. He closed the door and walked down the row. He stopped at the end and read the inscription: *Esperanza de la Cruz, 1974-2004.* After placing the flowers in front of the marble stone, he knelt to pray silently. When he was finished, he spoke to Esperanza directly.

After an hour he stood up and kissed the top of her headstone. *I'll visit you again soon. I love you.*

Hector and Scott rode in silence to the airport. As they entered the departures area, Scott released his seat belt and handed Hector some money for his effort.

"That is not necessary. Please, I cannot accept it," Hector said.

"Ok, thank you Hector. I appreciate everything. Will you please give my regards to the rest of the staff?"

"Absolutely, they ask about you all the time."

"Thanks."

"Scott, I want you to know that I never saw Esperanza as happy as she was when she was with you. I just wanted you to know that."

Scott felt a lump in his throat, but held it back. Hector came from a humble background, but had the sensitivity and manners of a prince. "Gracias, Hector. I appreciate it."

As Scott closed the door Hector asked, "What will you do now?"

Scott slung his bag over his shoulder, shook Hector's hand through the window and stood up straight. He exhaled and smiled before he answered. "I'm heading to D.C. for now. I start a new job tomorrow."

From the author

Thank you for your support, I hope you enjoyed this book. If you did, please recommend it to a friend. Also, I appreciate all reader feedback and can be reached through my website.

The Xpatriot is an independently published work, please help spread the word.

-RHM

www.randallhmiller.com

0-595-33153-X